The Forgotten Struggle

A Great War book

by Ryan Massmann

ISBN 978-1-7349440-0-6

Printed in the U.S.A. by
Smith Printing, LLC
Ramsey, MN 55303
(800) 416-9099 • www.smithprinting.com

This book is dedicated to the fallen of World War One,
to all of the children who suffered or died due to poverty,
abuse, and neglect, and to my parents,
John and Melissa Massmann.

Table of Contents

Chapter 1

The Great War Begins

The headlines in every paper throughout Germany read: "Archduke Franz Ferdinand and his wife Sophie have been assassinated today on June 28th, 1914. Serbian nationalist Gavrilo Princip is believed to be their assassin. The crime was committed in Sarajevo, Bosnia."

How could Serbia do such a thing? Hans Fitzgerald wondered after reading the news. Surely, they weren't trying to start a war? Or were they, and if they were, who would declare war first? Would Germany join the Austro-Hungarian Empire in the war if it started? These thoughts, and many others, crowded Hans's mind as he walked into the factory where he worked. His job was to make German zeppelins. The zeppelin they were building, the *Z 1X Zeppelin*, was going to be used to bomb France. Hans didn't completely understand why he needed to build it; the only thing he knew was that it was not for civilian use. Hans met up with his best friend, Carl.

“Guten morgen, Hans,” exclaimed Carl.

Hans happily shook Carl’s hand and replied, “Guten morgen to you as well, my friend.” But Hans was still very distracted, for those headlines had disturbed him to his very core. “Did you see the headlines today, the ones about the Archduke?” Hans asked.

“Not yet, Hans, but tell me, what has the Archduke gotten himself into this time?” Carl questioned.

“The news isn’t good,” Hans confessed, “not good at all.”

“Well, freund, what is it?” Carl asked.

“He’s dead, Archduke Franz Ferdinand is dead, and his wife too,” Hans sadly explained.

“Oh, mein Gott!” Carl cried, “wer hat es getan?”

“The man’s name is Gavrilo Princip, from Serbia,” Hans revealed.

“Mehr sagen,” Carl demanded.

“I’m sorry Carl, but I need to get to work, the zeppelin won’t build itself,” Hans added before running to the unfinished zeppelin. Hans gazed up at the skeleton of the zeppelin in all of its glory. It was like an oval-shaped balloon. But, unlike any other balloon, inside its borders a maze of beams and supports kept the frame together.

All over the zeppelin ladders leaned on the beams while people climbed them, risking their lives to build something they didn’t understand. Hans was one of those men, and so was Carl. Carl was on a prototype ladder made by Great Britain, but nobody had bothered to tell him. He was at the top of the ladder when Hans heard a loud SNAP.

The ladder buckled, and Carl plummeted toward the ground. Hans, working next to Carl, was too late to realize what was happening. He watched in horror as Carl hit the ground headfirst with a sickening crunch.

"Nein, nein, nein, nein, nein!" Hans screamed.

He climbed down the ladder, sobbing the whole way, "WARUM! CARL! WARUM!" he yelled as he ran to his best friend's side. One look and he knew his friend was dead. Blood gushed out of Carl's head –the wound was so big; everyone could see his cracked skull. Most of the workers vomited all over themselves at the gruesome sight. Hans fell to his knees and silently sobbed.

All of a sudden, a worker named Gustav called out by the broken ladder, "Boys, take a look at this." Everyone ran to him, and Gustav pointed to the bottom of the ladder.

"Right here, it says the ladder is a prototype made in Great Britain," he accused.

Everyone broke into hushed conversations, everyone except for Hans. He continued to look at the ladder, pure hatred in his eyes.

"I will get revenge on the British and all who have befriended them; if it's the last thing I ever do!" he yelled.

Soon everyone was vowing vengeance against Great Britain and their allies.

A few hours later, Hans was finished with work and had returned to his small middle-class home in Berlin,

Germany. He sat at his tiny wooden desk, his head in his hands, and thought of how his life used to be. He thought of his life in Ulm as a young child. His father, Alwin, and his mother, Gertrud, had just been divorced, and a young Hans was forced to leave his mother, never to see her again. His father had been building a new worktable, but, as he was pounding in a rusty nail, the hammer slipped, and the nail went into his hand. Hans heard his father scream but was too young to understand what it meant. A week later, Alwin's hand had a large, rotting hole in it. His father patched it up, saying he was fine, but couldn't get out of bed, and a few days later, he was dead. Hans had been put on a train and sent to Berlin as an orphan. His mother disowned him and wouldn't let Hans even see her. Before Hans arrived at the orphanage, he ran away and lived on the streets for many years. Even though he was a handsome young man, he still was unable to find a job; nobody wanted a homeless person working for them. Finally, a man named Carl took Hans into his home and gave him food and clothing. They soon became best friends, and Carl even found Hans the job at the zeppelin factory. Eventually, Hans was able to buy his own home, only a few blocks away from Carl's.

Shortly after, on a rainy day, Hans was walking home from work when he saw a young woman getting mugged by vicious gangsters. He knew what he had to do. He rushed to her defense and punched the first man in his face. The man fell over with a broken nose. Hans kicked the other man into a brick wall. He knocked the man unconscious with an uppercut. The woman said she was very grateful, and even though Hans was now dripping wet from the rain, he gave her his umbrella, for the gangsters had broken hers. Hans invited her to his home and they shared a hearty dinner. The woman said her name was Alice, and, after she left, Hans could not stop thinking about her dazzling blue eyes, her beautiful blonde hair tied into a tight bun, and her mesmerizing smile. It had been love at first sight. A few years later, they were married. Alice became pregnant with their first baby, who they were going to name Peter. But, out of nowhere, Alice fell ill with Typhoid Fever, and no one knew how to cure her. Everyone thought she would get better, but she never did. About a month before she would have given birth to Peter, Alice died along with her unborn child. Hans was crushed. But, no matter what happened, Carl was always there for him, whether they were laughing, crying, or shouting, he had always been there— until the accident. Now Hans had only himself. First, he lost his mother, then his father, his pride and dignity, his wife and only child, and now his best and only friend. Hans fell asleep at his desk, and, when he woke, it was morning. He ate a trifle bit of German sausage before heading off to work.

How will I ever be able to get revenge on Great Britain if they're so far away? he wondered and was about halfway to work before he remembered the war.

Maybe, he pondered, *if a war starts, Germany will join to help Austro-Hungary and Great Britain will join to help Serbia, which means I might actually get revenge on the British*.

He just had to wait and see if a war was going to start, and he didn't have to wait long. The Austro-Hungarian Empire declared war on Serbia on July 28th, 1914. But Germany did not become involved, yet. Because only two days after that, Russia began to mobilize its troops, which was an act of war. Germany had had enough and declared war on Russia on August 1st, 1914. Germany formed a plan that would call for a two-front war against Russia and its ally, France. But one country needed to be crossed for the Germans to attack France, Belgium. Germany issued an ultimatum insisting that the soldiers should be allowed to pass through Belgium. That was the final straw for the British, who then declared war on Germany. Hans had finally found the perfect opportunity to get even with the British and was one of the first Germans to join the war. The Great War, or World War 1, had begun.

Chapter 2
The First Battle of the Marne

Hans started his military career as part of the infantry, and his first mission was at the Battle of the Marne. A small group of soldiers, including Hans, were to find a way behind enemy lines and secure a bunker where French soldiers were using stolen German machine guns to attack the German lines. The chances were minimal that they would make it through what they called no man's land, but at least they had a small supply of smoke grenades

What if we could cover our advance with the grenades? Hans wondered. He explained his idea to the other soldiers and they agreed. Hans threw the grenades onto the wet and muddy ground. Soon, the grenades began to belch thick smoke, and the daring group of soldiers charged into no man's land. The plan worked at first, and the soldiers were almost to their goal, but when Hans looked up, he knew the detachment was doomed. The other soldiers looked up as well and watched as the smoke drifted away. The wind exposed every one of the grim soldiers. Machine-gun fire surrounded them. Hans desperately ordered them to advance. Their commander told them the opposite but was suddenly killed by German bullets.

First, they steal our weapons, and then they kill us with our own ammunition, Hans thought, shaking with anger. Hans and nine others managed to run into the trenches. But they weren't alone. Hans thrust the bayonet of his Gewehr 98 into an unsuspecting French soldier. The soldier screamed in agony as Hans pulled his bloody blade out of his gut. A few minutes later, the ten soldiers made it to the bunker. The French soldiers in the bunker were only armed with pistols, as the machine guns were stationary and took some time to move. There were four French soldiers, and they fought well, but were no match for the ten Germans. One French soldier grabbed his Pistole Revolveur Modele 1892 and shot Hans in the flesh above his shoulder. Hans yelled out but was still able to shoot the soldier right in his face. The fatally wounded soldier fell to the bloody ground, dead. Hans picked up the revolver. The other French soldiers were also on the ground, unmoving. The ten soldiers had secured the bunker at a huge cost. Out of the 30 or so soldiers that risked their lives to take that bunker, only ten survived. Hans and the others now had to clear the French trenches. Six of the Germans guarded the entrance while Hans and the other three fired the machine guns. The French didn't stand a chance as they were being killed from behind. The French soon lost so many men that the frontlines began to retreat.

A general in the German trenches blew his whistle and yelled, "OVER THE TOP BOYS!" which became one of the signature calls of the Great War. The other Germans saw the opportunity and began to charge through no man's land. The retreating French finally understood what had been killing them, and started to attack the bunker. Bullets screamed past Hans and his comrades. Hans, once again, felt doomed. Before he got to the ground for cover, he saw the bunker being lined with dynamite. "We need to get out of this..." Hans yelled but never finished as an ear-splitting explosion rocked the bunker, and he blacked out.

Hans woke an hour later. He saw double and couldn't feel anything. He came in and out of consciousness as a medic pulled him out of the concrete debris and brought him across no man's land. Hans woke up in a crowded green tent. He looked around and saw five of his comrades lying in the other beds. He also noticed a man lying in a bed next to him.

The man looked at Hans and asked, "What is your name?" Hans told the man his name and asked the same question.

The man replied, "my name is Adolf Hitler." Hans and Adolf became good friends as they lay wounded and recovering in their beds. A few days later, they were well enough to fight again. They were each given a new pickelhaube before going back to the trenches. Hans figured he would never see his new friend Adolf again, but he was very, very wrong. Hans learned that only five of his comrades survived the explosion. They had achieved their task at the expense of most of their force. Hans and his comrades were awarded the German Iron Cross for their heroic actions that day, but still, they wanted to fight in the Great War. This time, however, they were given something more powerful. Hans and his comrades walked to the military base and saw the strangest thing they had ever seen. It was a giant rectangle made of metal with treads on the bottom and machine guns on the sides.

"We call it the tank, the A7V tank, and you will be using it," the general said. Hans gazed in wonder at the remarkable machine of war and noticed something else. A massive gun was welded to the top of the tank. The back of the gun was in another metal box, which had a small slit in it.

"What is the gun on the top?" Hans asked.

"That is a 42cm kurze Marinekanone 14 L/12 artillery. We welded it to the top for more firepower; it is only experimental after all," the general answered.

"But isn't experimental weaponry unsafe?" Hans asked.

Surprised, the general asked, "Really, Hans? I thought you of all people would understand that war is dangerous. You did survive the journey through no man's land didn't you?" Hans had no response to the question. Suddenly, a dove landed on the general's shoulder. He untied a piece of paper from the dove's leg and read the hastily written message.

Trapped behind enemy lines! Section X 5, Y 20!
Tank captured! Come qui...

The rest of the message was covered with a splatter of blood.

"Boys, we need to go now! Get in the tank," he bellowed.

Hans and his crew ran to the tank. Hans quickly climbed up into the turret. One soldier named Fritz Fischer grabbed the driving controls and waited for it to start. Another named Frank Schwartz rotated the mechanism that started the tank. They both had been mechanics and knew a good deal about these machines. Frank then ran to a machine gun. The other three manned the other machine guns. Fritz started to drive the steel beast, and they were on their way. The rain that began earlier had become heavier, and the crew realized just how uncomfortable a tank was. It was cramped, and the team had no place to stretch their legs. The air was hot and heavy, and if their clothing got wet, it stayed wet. The whole tank already smelled of sweat and fuel. But Hans had the worst spot. Most of the heat and the smell wafted into the turret, and Hans felt sick. He tried to keep it down but eventually gave up. Vomit covered the turret. Some of it dripped down below, and the tank now had a new stench. The crew finally had to use one hand to plug their noses.

All of a sudden, Fritz yelled, "We got trenches up ahead! Prepare for battle!"

Chapter 3
A Rescue in Vain

Hans and his crew were oblivious to the fact that something more deadly lurked behind the trenches, artillery. The tank moved over the first trench, where the French had retreated when it stopped.

"She's not moving! Go find the problem, quick," Fritz yelled. They heard loud noises below the tank. Even Hans could hear them, and his memory told him what it was.

"Dynamite! They're lining her with dynamite," he yelled. He jumped out of the tank, wielding the revolver he had taken from the dead French soldier, and prepared to die. He saw the soldiers. They carried no weapons, but they had huge backpacks that were full of dynamite. One of them had the dynamite controls and only had to push down one mechanism to kill them all. They had shoved a thick log into the treads, preventing the movement of the tank. Hans shot the soldier with the controls in his hand. He dropped the controls to clench his now bloody hand. Another soldier pulled a Coupe Coupe machete from a sheath and lunged toward Hans. Hans screamed as he felt a sharp pain in his chest, and the blade bounced off one of his ribs. Hans barely managed to grab the machete from the soldier, but he did. He stabbed the soldier in the neck and yanked the machete back out. The man grabbed his neck tightly before staggering a few feet and falling. Hans quickly killed the other soldier before he could process what had happened. The dead man's hand was still twitching after Hans removed every piece of dynamite he saw. He left the controls there, knowing that nobody would be daft enough to use controls wired to live dynamite. He got back into the tank and bandaged his wound with some of the medical supplies. Hans also removed the log, and the tank was on its way.

They were almost behind enemy lines when they heard a loud WHOOSH. A large shell was launched into the gloomy sky, and it was heading straight for their tank. Fritz drove the tank as fast as he could, but he couldn't avoid the shell. It landed to the left of the tank, and the huge explosion covered them in wet mud. The tank started to lean toward the newly formed crater. Luckily, Fritz's driving skills kept them on the path of the unknown. Soon, they heard something else. It sounded like a giant orchestra consisting of only the loudest drums ever made. It was eight batteries of artillery, all firing shells at their single tank. The artillery's only flaw was that it was too late. By the time the shells hit the ground, the tank was far enough away to be unscathed by the deadly bombardment. But the noise made the entire crew's ears ring for hours. Hans took a look at the devastation behind them, and his jaw dropped. The crater was almost as big as the zeppelin he had been building, and it was nine feet at the deepest part. Hans saw the artillery in the distance and hoped that they could make it through alive. Suddenly, they veered to the left.

"What's going on, Fritz," Hans yelled.

"We're going to destroy the artillery before our luck runs out," Fritz yelled back.

"But, what about the rescue?" Hans asked.

"There will be no rescue if we get killed," Fritz shouted.

So, they kept approaching the artillery, though the chances were slim that they would survive. The crew started to fire the machine guns at the French soldiers manning the artillery.

"We are in range, Hans! Fire that gun," Fritz hollered.

Hans saw what looked to be slices of a gigantic shell and realized something. The dove had given its message to the general before they had learned how to use their weapons. Fritz and Frank were mechanics, meaning they knew how to do their jobs. Hans had never fired a weapon of this size and never anything this complicated.

Hans turned to Fritz, "I…I don't know how to fire the gun." The artillery was turning toward them.

"Speak up!" Fritz demanded, even though he heard what Hans said, he was in denial.

"I don't know how to fire the gun!" Hans cried.

There was a tense silence before Fritz screamed, "Oh mein Gott Hans! Oh mein Gott!" The entire crew cringed as Fritz said this, and a silent tear ran down Hans's cheek. *I failed everyone, it's all my fault. I could have been a better child and saved Dad. I could have found a way to save Alice and Peter, and we could have had a good life together. I could have saved . . . I could have saved Carl. After all he did for me, I couldn't save him.*

The French were loading shells into the big guns. Hans silently called out to his friend. *Carl, I need one more favor; I need to know how to fire this weapon. I couldn't save you, but if you help me, I can save these men who have risked their lives to fight for good in this world of evil. So please, Carl, please help me.* Hans looked at the gun and thought they were going to die. He would die in this cold, hard tank with people he didn't know. He would never find true happiness in his miserable life, only loss. When he died, he would forever live with the scum of humanity, for he had never given, only taken.

All of a sudden, as if Hans had fired the gun billions of times, he was able to load the shell slices into the barrel, create the shell in the barrel, work the mechanism, and fire the gun. He even had time to plug his ears as the shell was fired. However, the rest of the crew, thinking the gun would never fire, didn't plug their ears. A noise, almost as loud as the recent bombardment they had barely managed to escape, exploded in their ears. The shell hit right in between the two batteries of artillery, and they saw a giant explosion that shattered the artillery, creating a volley of molten hot shrapnel that flew in all directions. It also put small holes in their tank, weakening the armor of their deadly machine of war. They noticed one of the French soldiers who had been manning the artillery crawling on the ground. Flames covered his entire body, and where his right leg should have been, there was only a bloody stump. Finally, the man gave up, and the fire consumed him. They now had six batteries to go. But Hans knew that the Germans in need would not last much longer, and so he thought of a plan. The artillery could track them if they had visuals. The artillery had not been able to hit them accurately when they couldn't see their target. But they would have hit their tank spot on, had he not blown them to bits. However, all tanks had something in case of capture, flares. Hans figured that they could blind the artillery with their flares and sneak away to rescue the Germans. The rest of the crew agreed, except for Frank, who showed a bit of skepticism.

"And what happens when we are returning to base, and the artillery gets visuals on us?" he demanded.

"They will have no idea where to look, and we will be out of sight when they learn where we are," Hans calmly replied. So they fired the flares all around the artillery and sped off. Finally, they saw the other tank. It was driving toward them. Hans figured that the crew had managed to hold off the French, and they could now return home. They began to drive to the base together. Their tank went first, and the friendly tank drove right behind them. It also had a large gun on the top, though smaller than theirs. The artillery never fired, so the plan must have worked. Hans looked at the tank, which had shovel dents all over it, and saw something strange. The tank had ropes hanging down the sides. The ropes were tied to corpses. Something was tied to the corpses' heads. Hans looked closely and discovered they were helmets with a golden eagle on the front and a spike on the top. They were pickelhaubes. Before he could think, the French tank fired its weapon.

Chapter 4

The Cave to Mutually Assured Death

Their tank had been hit in the back, nobody was hurt but there was now a gaping hole there. One more hit, and the engine would explode. Fritz was very creative with his cursing as he turned their tank around. The French tank fired once again, and there was now a hole in the side of their vehicle. They turned all the way around. Hans was finally ready to fire. Just like the first time, he was easily able to do the job, and he fired the shell. It slammed into the front of the tank, folding it inward. All that was left of the driver were his ankles and boots. The gunners jumped out of the now smoldering hunk of metal and tried to run away. But, their machine guns cut them down with ease. The man using the top gun jumped from the disabled tank with incredible grace, and, before he could be killed, took out a pistol, shot under the tank, and once again, everything turned to black for Hans.

Hans was shaken from unconsciousness by Wilhelm Schwehr, one of the four gunners. “Hans, you need to see this,” he whispered. Hans rubbed the inch thick bleeding welt he had acquired after their tank had fallen 15 feet down into an isolated cavern. The only way was forward. Hans looked at what Wilhelm wanted to show him and was blown away. The entire cavern was covered in a staggering assortment of unnaturally beautiful multicolored minerals. They were so beautiful that Hans could not resist gazing into them. For some reason, after all they had been through, Hans felt incredibly relaxed. As he walked closer, however, he started to feel very weak. He stumbled and fell to his knees.

Hans was walking in Berlin. He felt someone holding his hand, and he looked to his left. He saw Alice and remembered. They had been married for two years, and Alice was just a month away from giving birth to their first child. They were deciding what to name their baby.

“You said he was going to be a boy, right? I think we should name him Otto. I think it sounds like a proper name in a working-class family,” Hans said.

Alice shook her head, “What about Maximilian? I think it sounds very noble, like the country he will grow up in.”

Hans politely disagreed, “What about Arsenio? I once was talking to a rich French merchant, and he told me his name was Arsenio.”

Alice gasped, “Hans, you know that the kids in school will make fun of him if you name him that. What about Peter? That sounds more new and original than some of the other names out there.”

Hans thought for a moment before he happily replied, “Whatever you want, meine liebe, I don’t care what his name is, as long as you like it.”

“It doesn’t matter, as long as we are all together as a family,” Alice responded.

“We are so fortunate for our good health. I think we will live long lives together,” Hans said. And they said no more as they walked through the park, both full of life. Ironically, the next day Alice fell ill from Typhoid Fever, and she would never recover.

“HANS! SNAP OUT OF IT!” Wilhelm screamed after he slapped Hans so hard, tears welled up in Hans’s eyes.

“How long was I out?” Hans groggily asked.

“I have no idea,” said Wilhelm, “You seemed to be in some sort of semi-conscious state. You were talking, your eyes were rolled up in your head, and you kept breathing very deeply. I think the fumes in the air caused it. They seemed to be coming from the minerals because when I put you in the tank, you stopped acting so strangely. They seemed to be sapping at your sanity every minute while I was figuring out what to do.”

"I don't even remember waking up after that French soldier shot at our tank," Hans replied.

"Well, our comrades have tried to fix the tank, but we have no materials down here. We think that that soldier shot the bottom of the tank because you missed some of that dynamite the French put there," Wilhelm informed him. Their once incredible tank now had large holes on the side, the back, and on the bottom.

"Can she still be driven?" Hans asked.

"Yes," Wilhelm answered, "but the engine is quite damaged. It could blow at any moment." Soon, Hans was in the damaged turret, and Wilhelm, Frank, and the other gunners were at their dented posts, and Fritz was at the broken seat. Fritz started the engine. It sounded like nails on a chalkboard. Everyone shuddered at the unpleasant sound. Sparks flew from the engine, and it just barely kept working. The wheels were even worse. Both treads had been ripped off, and every single wheel had been slashed by the minerals. The fact that the tank could even move was extraordinary. It inched along the rough ground. The cavern kept getting smaller, and the sides of the tank began to scrape against the minerals. More sparks flew, and the whole crew tried to block out the shrill and piercing SCREECH. As they moved along, they moaned and screamed in utter agony. Their tank now had deep scars running from the front to the back. After what seemed like decades, they saw what appeared to be an enormous lake. But as they got closer, they noticed that the 'water' was very thick, greasy, and dark black. They noticed a tower made entirely of metal beams with a large oil rig attached to the middle of it. Hans had seen this tower before. The wealthy merchant had shown him a picture of it.

"Bonjour, amis, welcome to France," Hans said grimly. In about three seconds, Hans saw five muzzles point into the turret.

"If you didn't get the message, we are in France," Hans shouted into the tank. Hans now knew why the Eiffel tower existed. It was so the military could take useful resources for themselves. Nobody could stop cursing as Fritz drove them into a large alcove. The path up into Paris was wide because the French needed to bring large machines down to fix the rig if it was damaged. They used the ramp to drive slowly up to the light. They were now in the lion's den. The top of the tarp was covered with dirt, which had grass growing out of it. Paris was filled with pedestrians, all of whom were not happy to see a tank covered in iron crosses. It was like putting the symbol of anarchy into the middle of a peace-loving city. As luck would have it, there was a police station just a block away. They would soon have the authorities on their tails. Hans only had a small number of shells left. They had no place to run, and they were in the center of the country of their enemy. As if on cue, police automobiles drove in from the right. However, Hans chuckled, because as soon as the policemen saw their sad excuse of a tank, they quickly veered in the other direction. Hans now knew they had some time, and he jumped down into the main tank area.

"What does our engine need?" he asked Frank.

"The radiator is melted, the oil tank exploded, and the clutch snapped in half in that fall," Frank answered. After hearing this, Hans grabbed his Gewehr 98 from the weapons rack, put some grenades in a backpack, and went into the streets of Paris.

Paris was quite beautiful, despite the chaos. He ran down cobblestone streets, looking for the military base. Suddenly, a large convoy of Renault armored cars sped down the streets, heading towards the tank. Hans saw that the streets were small, and the motorcade traveled single file. That gave him an idea. If he destroyed the first vehicle, the convoy would have to waste some time to find a path around the wreckage.

If they see me, their machines will tear me apart. But they can't kill me if they can't see me. Hans grabbed a few smoke grenades and threw them at the convoy. The smoke shooting out of the canisters gave Hans memories of his very first mission with his comrades. Now, he was ready for action. He took a bundle of anti-tank grenades and threw them at the first vehicle, though he could hardly see it. They collided with the protective armor and exploded. The explosion blew the engine to pieces. The shockwave knocked Hans off his feet. He landed on his hand and heard a SNAP. It was the sound of his finger breaking. He yelled and held it up, but there was no time to take care of it. He moved quickly, hid in a building, and watched the convoy. The second car crashed into the first, causing it to blow up. The shrapnel broke the windows and put holes in the third vehicle's engine, so it stopped working. The sudden blockage of the road forced the remaining Renaults to stop. Hans had stopped the attack force, but it was only the first, reinforcements were probably on the way. Hans's hand was throbbing, but he had no medical supplies. There would be no relief from the pain and no time to rest. He knew what he had to do. Hans's next job was to infiltrate the military base.

Chapter 5
Hans vs. the Triple Entente

The base was only about eight blocks away. It was by the imposing Seine River, which led to the ocean. A massive British dreadnought, named the HMS Snow, sat in the water. The base was packed full of all types of machines and weapons. French guns and grenades lined the walls. A new and devastating weapon was being tested in the bowels of the base. It was called a flamethrower. A few ugly black masks lay on a bench. They had a canister on the bottom, and large spaces covered with a transparent substance where a person's eyes would be. There were also grenades by the masks that had a strange symbol on them. There were biplanes, triplanes, French tanks, motorbikes, Renaults, artillery of all ranges, field guns, AA guns, and horse stables. There was also a damaged A7V tank. Soldiers were everywhere. The only real advantage Hans had was the element of surprise and clothing. While Hans had a gray uniform, the French wore brightly colored blue uniforms with red pants, making them easy targets. Hans silently sneaked into the base and went to the bench. He put on one of the masks, scanning the pamphlet inside to learn how to do so. He grabbed several of the grenades and threw them. Hans would never forget what he saw that day. Instead of belching out smoke, the wind blew a green gas that flooded the area. The soldiers tried to escape but were unsuccessful. They all fell on the ground. They were screaming, writhing, and clutching their throats. Their eyes bugged out, and they kept coughing. In just a few seconds, they stopped moving. Corpses littered the hard floor as Hans walked forward. He took his Coupe Coupe and sliced one of the bodies open. He gasped and started to shake. The man's lungs were completely black and melted. Hans had just used a gas grenade, or, more specifically, a chlorine gas grenade. It was the first use of chemical warfare and one of the things that would make the Great War infamous. Three British soldiers ran up some stairs from the corner. One of them held a Martini-Henry rifle, and the other two had a flamethrower. The man in the back wore a circular metal tank on his back, while the one in the front sneered and aimed the nozzle of the weapon of death and destruction. Hans was barely able to lunge behind a howitzer as sinister red flames burst out the nozzle. Just as he was about to be spotted, Hans hid under the howitzer. The soldiers looking for him, walked around taunting and insulting him. They said things like, "Oy, George! They told me that them Jerry's were supposed to be brave," and, "If you fought better than you could hide,

Fritz, we would all be dead." But Hans was too smart to fall for their jabs. He had dealt with people like this before on the streets of Berlin. They were often so self-assured that they took deadly risks. Hans rolled a gas grenade toward one of them. The man didn't see where it came from, but wasn't fazed by it. He picked it up, laughed, and put his gas mask on. The others did the same, and nobody was hurt. However, this was all part of Hans's plan. He rolled another grenade almost identical to the first out toward the group. The cruel man picked up the second grenade, too busy laughing to realize he wasn't holding a gas grenade this time. They didn't even have time to scream. Three mangled bodies hit the floor. Hans realized what he needed to do. He grabbed dynamite from his backpack and rigged it to as many of the vehicles as he could. *The explosions should cause a chain reaction that will bring the entire base down,* Hans thought. It was ready, but he still had one more thing to do. He jumped into the damaged A7V and examined the complicated controls as quickly as he could. He had no choice; he had to drive it. Hans figured out how to move forward and turn just as some soldiers ran out of the docked dreadnought. It seemed they had heard the commotion at the base, and knew that someone had stolen one of their tanks. They were each carrying a long rifle. One of the men grabbed a large shell from a satchel. Though Hans couldn't see it, writing on the shell read *Anti-Tank Shell* in French. He loaded the shell and fired his rifle. A loud splintering crack sounded to Hans's right and, to his amazement, the shell blasted a hole in the tank's armor. Hans was so frightened that he nearly fell off the seat. He accidentally placed his left hand on the dynamite control. The explosion sent deadly shrapnel flying in all directions. Suddenly, the skeleton of a French tank smashed into Hans's captured A7V, knocking it onto its side. Hans smashed his head on the engine, but felt uninjured. Knowing the tank would not bring him any farther, he detached the parts he needed and abandoned it. The parts were heavy in his backpack, and his vision was blurry, but he forged onward. He was about halfway to his tank when his left hand spasmed in pain. He suddenly remembered his broken finger. The adrenaline rush that had filled him kept him from feeling the pain until now. His head had been wounded earlier and started to ooze blood. It trickled down Hans's handsome face like molasses. He was now only a block away from his tank when a civilian pulled a pistol from his tattered jacket and aimed it at Hans's head. Hans tried to grab his own pistol, but the man fired. Hans fell to the ground, blood dripping from the wound. But he was not dead. Hans was left-handed, so he tried to grab his pistol with his left hand,and as he did so, he flinched in pain from his broken finger. The man had fired at the same time, and the bullet only grazed his ear lobe. The civilian fled, and Hans made it to the A7V. Wooden planks covered the large holes. The dilapidated remains of Renaults littered the town square. Bullet sized dents dotted the entire tank, but it had survived the onslaught. Hans opened the right hatch and climbed in it. The crew looked pale and gaunt, their faces showing their exhaustion. Wilhelm saw Hans and grinned.

"You have the luck of the devil, Hans. Heinrich was not so lucky, however." He gestured to a makeshift bed in the back of the tank, where the crew member lay. He was riddled with bullet holes; a sizable bandage was tightly wrapped around his right arm, soaked with blood.

"What happened to his arm?" Hans quietly asked.

"We think the bullet pierced his basilic vein," Wilhelm answered. Heinrich was still alive, but his skin was the color of alabaster, and he was unconscious.

"How did he get shot so many times?" Hans asked.

"We had hardly any shells to fire, and our other weapons can't pierce the Renault's armor. Heinrich jumped out of the tank with some grenades, and ran to a Renault, opened the top hatch, and threw the grenades in. He was shot many times, but managed to kill the entire crew, all by himself. He climbed into the Renault and used it to destroy all eight vehicles. He used dynamite to destroy his Renault, so it could not be captured," Wilhelm replied.

Hans was speechless as he realized how brave Heinrich was.

The French, the British, and the Serbians painted Germany and its people as monsters— people who only fought for the 'wrong side'. War is not black and white. It's not about fighting for 'good' or 'bad'. It's about fighting for what you believe is right. Heinrich nearly died fighting to save his friends. Hans decided that he would take care of Heinrich while the crew worked. The turret only had a small number of shells, so they needed to be rationed. Hans would go into the turret if they ran into serious trouble. Heinrich was nearly dead, but Hans removed the remaining bullets from his battered body and stopped the bleeding as best he could. However, Hans had forgotten about one crucial thing.

"Hans! Those civilians know we are weak. We need to leave Paris now. You must have done some scouting. Where are we heading?" Fritz yelled.

Hans had one idea, but it would take some convincing.

Chapter 6
The HMS Snow

"So let me get this straight," Fritz said in a tone of disbelief, "You want to go *toward* the enemy and sneak into a heavily armed dreadnought?"

"Would you rather travel through half of France? This tank won't last that long, even with our improvised repairs. The French won't destroy their own dreadnought; they're very cautious about using their naval power," Hans answered sternly.

"We have no idea where that ship will take us. There may be hundreds of crew members on board," Fritz countered.

"That military base had a damaged A7V. Our tank is also damaged. All we need to do is falsely signal to the French that the tank is captured and drive aboard," Hans informed.

Fritz decided that they had no other choice, and they started toward the warship. They agreed to take a longer route than the one Hans used, as his original way was packed with vehicle remains. After a long and stress-filled half of an hour, they finally reached the HMS Snow. It was specially designed with a smaller bottom to navigate the Seine. It had four large turrets, each equipped with two 20mm cannons. The sides were painted blue, green, and yellow while in the center, a 1850s pump was painted with the grim reaper coming out of the nozzle. The armor was eight inches thick. It looked indomitable. The military base was completely destroyed, thanks to the bravery of Hans Fitzgerald. The clearing was a graveyard of mutilated vehicles and machines. Fire grasped the ruins of the once glorious base. The flamethrower, the gas masks and grenades, and the plans for a new British tank were all destroyed, and would not be used until much later in the Great War.

The tank crawled towards the HMS Snow, a pirate symbol painted on the dented front. The captain, who had been drinking a little too much champagne during all of the commotion, was passed out as the A7V drove right into the open hatch of the ship. The HMS Snow was to carry vehicles back to the trenches and was about to leave. The inside of the menacing dreadnought was quite small, and filled with British and French soldiers. Fritz drove their A7V by a few other vehicles and stopped. At first, all seemed normal. Everyone ignored the tank, but then the mechanics came. These mechanics also happened to be medics, so they had medical supplies. The mechanics knew that the tank needed a crew, but they didn't see anyone.

Hans and the rest of his team were hoping to hide the fact that they were Germans. The mechanics knocked on the dented hatches, waiting for a reply. There was none. The first of the frustrated mechanics climbed in the tank. Hans decided that he would deal with him. When the man came in from the right hatch, Hans simply wrapped his muscular arm around the thin neck of the unsuspecting man, exposed his jugular vein, and slit his throat with his bloodstained Coupe Coupe. Hans had begun to adore the well balanced and sharp French melee weapon. Hans took the clothing off the corpse and carried the dead man to the back of the tank. The rest of the crew had carefully concealed themselves during this, knowing that their discovery would be detrimental to Hans's plan. Hans climbed out of the tank and walked to the other mechanic. The man looked at Hans strangely, as if something was a bit off. During Hans's training in Germany, he had learned a bit of the French language in his spare time, knowing it may come in handy.

"Where is the driver of this tank, Louis?" the mechanic asked.

"I need to talk to you in private," Hans answered in a mediocre French accent, and the confused mechanic raised a thin eyebrow. Hans walked through a maze of passages and hallways, most of them filled with British or French soldiers. The mechanic knew that Hans was both an imposter and a skilled fighter. He had a gut feeling Hans had killed Louis, but told no one. His family had forced him to become a mechanic, knowing it was not nearly as dangerous as being a soldier. He made the mistake of telling the crew about it when he joined. In mere days, he was a laughingstock. He wanted glory. He wanted to deal with this stealthy infiltrator by himself and prove his worth. So, as Hans was leading him around the corner, he pulled an old rag and a bottle of chloroform out of his kit. Chloroform was used as a type of anesthesia during World War 1, and many medics used it. The mechanic put some chloroform on the rag, grabbed a rope, and waited. Hans finally got to a point where five hallways intersected. He scratched his head and put his hands behind his back, trying to decide which hall to go down. The mechanic walked right behind Hans and made his move. He slammed Hans onto the ground, hastily tied the thick rope around his struggling hands, turned him over and put the rag over his nose and mouth. Hans continued to struggle in vain, he could hardly breathe, and the short battle was lost. Everything faded into darkness, and his eyes rolled up into his head as he lost consciousness.

Hans awoke in a rectangular room. The ceiling was arched, but the room was only about six and a half feet tall at the highest point. A small, filthy toilet stained with urine and feces sat in the corner and to the left of it sat a broken cot with a sliced up pillow, revealing that rocks were used as stuffing. Hans tried to stand, but a splitting headache forced him back down. The pain ricocheted through his head, causing him to writhe and yell out in agony. After several minutes, the pain eased. He slowly stood up, but still felt a bit light-headed and woozy. He got his bearings and realized that he was in a jail cell. The cramped, concrete room made Hans feel claustrophobic. The memory of what had happened came back to him, *how could I have been so stupid? I failed my entire crew. I have embarrassed the Germanic people and our Austro-Hungarian allies. Our entire philosophy is to be strong and obedient in the face of danger. Our German soldiers are the best in Europe. How was I defeated by a mere mechanic?* Hans felt a mix of despair, embarrassment, and shame. The feeling of failure— the dread he felt after being unable to fire the tank shell— once again plagued him. He sat on the revolting cot, trying to formulate a plan when he heard two British men talking about him.

"So, thi...this Jerry in the cage, what we go...gonna do 'bout him?" the first man asked. His voice had a higher pitch, and he seemed to stutter frequently.

"We gonna shoot him in a couple hours, we jus' need to check his records, think he's a landship Jerry though," the second answered. His voice sounded smooth yet deep, like a brass instrument. Hans turned pale, his hands became clammy, and he started shaking. He knew from Fritz that the British were brutal to crew members of tanks. His only hope was his crew, but they had no idea where he was.

Meanwhile, the A7V was being searched. The crew was still hiding, but that wouldn't last much longer. The HMS Snow was headed for the English Channel, where it would pick up supplies from Britain. The ship would then head for the Marne, where the supplies would be brought to the ongoing battle. The soldiers searching the tank took everything except the weapons, which the crew had with them. The A7V would most likely be used for scrap or research.

The Germans had discovered British blueprints of the 'landship' or the 'tank' as it would later be called. German mechanics looked it over and sought to improve upon the flawed design. They created the A7V tank. Before they realized how expensive their model was, they manufactured five with the 42cm kurze Marinekanone 14 L/12 artillery gun mounted on the top.

The British captured A7V tanks to research their flaws and strengths, so they would no longer be a threat to the Triple Entente. The French had barely stopped the well trained German army at the Marne with only two A7Vs to deal with, but somehow, without those tanks, the Germans were losing momentum. Many of the major countries were using conscription— If men met certain requirements, they were obligated to fight— and it gave these countries the vast armies that would make history. It also led to high casualties on both sides. The French knew that if Paris was captured, they would have a much lower chance of winning the war. Germany would focus all its troops on

Russia, which would directly correspond with the Schlieffen Plan (the plan that called for the two-front war)—when Russia was knocked out of the war, Britain would have no choice but to surrender to Germany and its allies. However, the French held on to France. Better tanks would greatly help the French at the Marne. The crew's tank would be of extraordinary use to France at the moment, especially with the mounted artillery. But for the crew, the tank was of no use. If they blasted a hole in the ship, they were doomed. When the crew realized Hans wouldn't be returning, they assumed the worst. They figured he was dead, but they had no time to grieve. They had a plan, one that would lead to either their demise or their rescue.

Chapter 7
Blood and Steel

Hans heard noises outside his prison door before it swung open to reveal a large, bulky and extremely muscular man.

"Hans Fitzgerald," the man said, his voice matching the deep one he had heard outside his cell. "Instead of simply executing you, as was planned, we decided, bein' you caused us all dis' trouble at Marne and Paris, we gonna have a little fun with you first."

Hans felt the urge to vomit. He knew that by fun they meant brutal torture practices that they learned from the Russians. It was so inhumane that only a few were punished in this way. The man put handcuffs around Hans's wrists, and dragged him away.

The crew realized that a majority of the troops had left the tank, allowing them to escape. They all took out their standard-issue Luger PO8 pistols. What followed was an all-out standoff. The crew was outnumbered three to one, but they had two things to their benefit— more experience and the element of surprise. The British and French men were caught entirely off guard, having searched the tank and not finding them, and they didn't expect an ambush. In a few seconds, Wilhelm killed three men with three rounds and three headshots. Fritz shot a surprised soldier in his heart. Frank shot at a soldier, but only hit his knee, shattering the kneecap into splinters. The soldier fired one last round before falling. Frank corrected the first shot, shooting the fallen man in his skull, killing him instantly. Heinrich jumped behind an armored car; the soldier he was fighting was firing his revolver at a maximum rate. When the soldier stopped to reload, Heinrich peeked around the corner, and put a bullet in the man's forehead. The sixth man of the crew, Herman, had picked up one of the French revolvers using it and the PO8 at the same time, one in each hand. He fired both at their maximum rate at the four men. Within a few seconds, they were all on the ground, peppered with bullet holes. At this point, the floor was a mess of blood and gore. Now it was equal, five Germans to five Britons. The French had all been killed, their vibrant blue uniforms making them easy targets. The five Britons retreated behind cover, shooting at the crew from afar with Lee-Enfield rifles. The crew all took out their Gewehr 98s, except for Wilhelm, who used a Mauser Model 1871, which he had acquired from the First Samoan Civil War. Out of all the crew, Wilhelm was the only war veteran, which is why he was such an exceptional marksman. Wilhelm went off to the side, aimed his Mauser, and took the first man down. Fritz and Frank each shot a man at almost the same time. Heinrich shot a man in the head, but the soldier had also fired a shot. The bullet carved a long gash in Heinrich's cheek. There was only one man left. They all aimed for him, and they all fired at once. Five holes appeared in the man's face before he fell over backward. They all cheered, except for Frank. He was holding his gut. His hands covered in blood. The soldier Frank had encountered had successfully hit him. He stumbled, his face pale. Herman caught Frank before he fell. The crew crowded around Frank, panicking. Herman gently lay Frank down on the floor. Fritz ran to get medical supplies from the tank but realized too late that they had been taken. Herman took Frank's shirt off and searched for the bullet that was lodged in his gut. After some time, he pulled out the blood-soaked bullet. Frank's stomach was decimated in several places. Heinrich ripped some cloth from the uniforms of the corpses. He ran to Frank, using the fabric to cover the wound. They all knew that the bleeding would have to be stopped quickly, or Frank would die. Frank was unconscious due to shock and blood loss. He wouldn't last much longer.

Hans was in a large room, with at least a hundred soldiers surrounding him. They all had knives. The man that had handcuffed him took off Hans's shirt, and tied him by the waist and wrists to a wooden post. Hans faced the post with his back exposed to the soldiers.

The man stepped back and shouted to the soldiers, “Go get ‘em, boys!” The soldiers ran to Hans, knives at the ready. When the soldiers got to Hans, they started carving. They ripped through Hans’s back, running their blades through his flesh. In a matter of minutes, Hans’s back was a myriad of torn and severed flesh, blood cascading down all of it. He screamed in absolute agony. He was extremely close to passing out from the pain. Hans heard a gunshot, and the cutting stopped. The shot was fired by the person who handcuffed him.

“Winston, we were having fun,” one soldier complained.

“Shut that filthy mouth a yours, Johnny!” Winston angrily replied.

Johnny shook his head and walked into the crowd.

“Now,” he continued, “We gonna let ‘em stand there all night.” Half of the soldiers laughed, the other half complained, but all of them insulted Hans. Winston led the soldiers out of the room, leaving Hans to suffer.

“There,” Wilhelm informed. He had cut a sliver of bone from a French corpse and tied it to some string. He used this to sew Frank’s wound together. Frank still needed serious medical treatment, but he wouldn’t die just yet. Now the plan could be set into motion. They just had to reach the communications post. Together, they decided that Wilhelm and Herman would find the post, while Heinrich and Fritz would stay with Frank. So Wilhelm and Herman left. They knew that they needed to rewire the communications post to send telegrams to Germany, and then find the telegraph room. Rewiring the post would be key because if the telegram was sent to Britain, they would never escape the ship. They also knew that the communications post was at the top of the ship. They didn't have to walk far before finding a ladder leading to the deck. They both climbed up and looked for the post. It was drizzling, making the deck slippery. There was one problem; however, at least eight guards were walking on the deck. They patrolled the area, wearing plates of armor on their chests, arms, and legs. Each of them held a trench mace in one hand, and a cut-down LeeEnfield in the other. After some searching, Wilhelm saw the post. They used another ladder to get to the top area of the ship. Herman started to climb up the exposed ladder, and Wilhelm was about to follow when he slipped, banging his chin on the ladder. The guards saw them and fired a few rounds, but missed, mainly because their Enfields were cut-down, giving them decreased accuracy. They also lacked a scope. One of the guards yelled something, and three guards went after Wilhelm and Herman. Wilhelm got up and hastily climbed up the ladder. The three guards were almost to the top platform. The rain began to fall in sheets now, decreasing visibility and making the ladder slippery. Wilhelm and Herman struggled to climb the ladder, coming extremely close to falling to a brutal death several times. The guards started to climb the ladder. Wilhelm pulled out his PO8 and shot at one of the guards. However, the bullet simply bounced off his metal chest armor. The guard aimed his Enfield, blowing off the top of Wilhelm's ring finger. Wilhelm yelled as blood splattered his gray uniform. He then aimed his PO8 and shot the guard's hand. He lost his grip and fell off the ladder, knocking another guard down with him. There was now only one guard left on the ladder. He took aim, his sights on Wilhelm's head. BAM. The guard fell off the ladder. Wilhelm looked up. Herman's gun was smoking. He shot the guard in his exposed head. Wilhelm was about to thank Herman but realized they had to achieve their goal first. They finally reached the top of the ladder and saw a transmitter. Herman took out his trench knife and cut the transmitter open. He found the two main wires and cut the green one. He knew that every message went to Britain. They knew that if their message reached Britain, escape would be impossible. Now, all messages would only go to the desired country. Herman and Wilhelm began their treacherous journey down the ladder. Fog rolled in, causing limited visibility. The guards continued to fire blindly. They had no idea where Herman and Wilhelm were. If they sent more guards to fight them, they could risk shooting their own men. Herman and Wilhelm reached the bottom. They retraced their route, and just before they descended into the ship, a guard smoking a cigarette spotted them. He yelled to the other guards, and they ran toward Herman and Wilhelm. Wilhelm desperately looked for a way to the bottom of the ship. He spotted a stairway leading down. He and Herman ran as fast as they could down the stairs.. Drops of blood from Wilhelm's hand left a path for the guards to follow. Wilhelm wasn't thinking about his hand at the moment. He kept trying to find staircases leading down. Soon, they reached a hallway and ran down it, checking the signs over each door, Wilhelm on the left, Herman on the right.

Eventually, Herman yelled, "Right here!" They opened the door and ran to the telegraph machine. Wilhelm locked the door.

Herman typed on the telegraph:

SOS! Germans stuck on ship in English Channel.
Need ship big enough to carry A7V tank. May need
1 or 2 U-boats. Coordinates are unknown.

Just as he finished, he heard a gunshot. Smoke curled from the door as the twisted lock fell off. Wilhelm quickly fired five shots into the door. He heard two bodies drop. The other three guards kicked open the door and took out their trench maces. Herman shot a guard in his forehead, and he dropped his mace. Herman grabbed the mace and hit a guard in the head with it. The man fell over, half of his face caved in and bleeding. Wilhelm shot the other man between his eyes. They just had to get back to the others, which was relatively simple, now that the path was clear and they could retrace their steps. They told everyone what had happened, and explained that they just had to wait. One thing they didn't understand was where all of the other soldiers were.

Hans hung from the post, barely able to stand for what felt like a lifetime. Suddenly, an explosion shook the entire ship. Soldiers were running and cursing in a panic, and the alarm was sounding. As someone ran past him, their knife fell out of its leather sheath and landed about an arms-length from Hans. Hans's wrists were tied to the post, but he had an idea. He dropped down and used his right leg to bring the knife in between his legs. Hans brought his hands down and picked it up. He cut his wrists loose and then his waist. Amidst the chaos, nobody even noticed him. He started to run, looking for the last place he saw his crew. After a few minutes, he found the front of the boat. He saw the A7V driving off the front ramp and onto another boat. He also saw something beside the boat.

Oh, no, he thought, as he gazed at the U-boat. In any other situation, Hans would be delighted to see a U-boat, but there was just one problem, he was on the target of the submarine. The sub fired another missile, knocking Hans off his feet. He hit his head on the metal floor. Once Hans got back up, he felt nauseous and staggered to the front of the now sinking dreadnought. He knew he had to get off the ship; however, he could hardly see straight, and vomit filled his throat. His biggest problem was that he couldn't get to the front of the boat fast enough. Vomit dribbled out of his mouth and onto the floor, and he almost blacked out again, but he had to keep going. Once he got close to the front ramp, he saw a panicking French guard firing at the German boat and he ducked behind a crate. He pulled out the knife and walked slowly to the guard so he could stealthily take him out. Otherwise, it would be impossible to get to the other boat. He was close to the man when he suddenly turned around. Hans stabbed him in the neck, killing him instantly. He then started to sprint as fast as he could. The boat was leaving, and he was too late. Hans would have to jump to get onto the boat. He prepared himself, took a step back, ran forward, and jumped.

Chapter 8

The Dangerous Rescue of the A7V

Hans just barely caught the edge of the boat, while struggling to pull himself up he was forced to drop the Browning Model 1910 into the icy water below, so, once again, he only had his knife. The deck of the ship was swimming with guards surrounding the A7V. Hans was relieved when he saw that the rest of his crew was safe. He saw them climbing out of the tank and staggered toward them. When they noticed Hans, they were awestruck. None of them could believe they were all still alive, and their shock quickly turned to joy.

"We thought you were dead," said Fritz, but he also noticed how weak Hans looked. "What did they do to you?"

"We can discuss that over abendessen," Hans answered. Hans watched a group of men carry Frank's limp body out of the tank, and his heart sank. Frank, covered in blood, looked close to death. Hans ran to the men carrying Frank and asked if he would be okay. They told him Frank would be taken care of and treated well.

Hans and the rest of the crew went below decks and sat down at an elegant spruce table laden with bread, potatoes, kohlrabi, and schnapps. Once Hans saw the food his hunger took over. He inhaled the kohlrabi and drank a small glass of schnapps.

Everyone ate in ravenous silence for a few minutes until Fritz spoke. "Hans, what did they do to you?"

Hans told everyone the story, and when he finished, everyone had lost their appetites.

"Thank goodness they were cruel," Wilhelm said. Everyone stared at him like he was insane.

"What do you mean?" Fritz asked.

"What I mean is if they weren't so cruel as to torture Hans, they would have executed him, and he wouldn't be sitting with us right now." Everyone looked at him and realized that he was right.

"What happened to Frank?" Hans asked.

"He was shot during a firefight," Wilhelm answered gravely.

"Is he alive?" Hans asked nervously.

"We don't know yet, but he was in bad condition when we last saw him, and the doctor said that it would take quite some time for him to recover from the gunshot wound," Fritz answered. Shortly after Fritz finished speaking, the doctor walked into the room to give them an update on Frank.

"Frank went into a potentially fatal coma, but I managed to extract the bullet from him. He should recover if he comes out of his coma, but I don't think he will be able to fight for a while. There is a good chance that he will be okay, but I can't make any promises."

"That's a relief," Hans said optimistically.

Hans realized that he hadn't slept for a long time, and exhaustion overtook him. He dragged himself into the sleeping quarters of the ship and slept deeply for several hours.

When he woke up, all of his friends were already in the kitchen, eating breakfast.

Herman raved about how good his eggs, sausage, and sauerkraut soup were compared to the canned beef and other canned foods they would have to get used to having day in and day out again. Once they finished eating, they all went to the front of the ship's deck and watched it slice through the water. Suddenly a siren went off, and they gave each other a knowing look. The siren meant that a submarine had been spotted, and all the crew members had to get to their battle stations to prepare for a strike, or they would sink. All of a sudden, the boat turned sharply to the right. Hans, Fritz, and Wilhelm were swept off of their feet. They all heard something moving toward the ship from the water, and they knew what it was. The destroyer turned again to the right. A missile flew right past the front of the destroyer. They had narrowly escaped the jaws of death.

They looked around for the sub, but suddenly there was a huge explosion to their left. Twisted metal flew at least 30 feet into the air. The U-boat that was accompanying them had fired a torpedo at the enemy sub, destroying it. About an hour after the incident it was back to normal. A bell rang notifying the crew that they had thirty-five minutes to eat lunch. If they missed mealtime, they didn't eat. They had canned beef, biscuits, and bread, and Wilhelm was regaling them with his past war experiences when Hans thought of something.

"What port are we going to?" he asked.

A crew member next to him replied, "Zeebrugge."

"Isn't that in Belgium?" Hans asked.

"Yes, it is. This destroyer lacks the fuel to return to Germany. We had to use extra fuel to extract you from that British ship. Our destroyer has been patrolling the channel for a while, so Zeebrugge will have to do," the man replied. Hans decided to check on Frank. However, upon reaching the small medical room, he was stopped by the doctor.

"Frank is still in a coma, I'm afraid. So I cannot permit you to enter this room," he said crossly.

"Frank is my friend. I have every right to see him. It's what he would want," Hans stubbornly replied.

"No. It will only take him longer to recover if you cause him stress."

"You can't stop me," Hans said.

The doctor sighed, "I guess you're right." He gestured inside, "enter."

Hans walked in and saw Frank. He was pale, and his gut was covered in bandages soaked in iodine. "So, have you stopped all the bleeding?" Hans inquired.

"Internally, yes. Externally, no. I think he should be out of the coma tomorrow," replied the doctor.

"Good, but you *cannot* let him die between now and then. I've lost too much, and I don't want to lose another one," Hans begged.

"What do you mean another one?" the doctor asked.

"Well..."

Hans told the doctor how he lost his friend Carl, who allowed him to have food, water, and a place to stay. He also told him about how he lost his wife and his son to Typhoid Fever.

"I am very sorry for you. I will try my best to keep him alive," The doctor comforted.

"At least now I know that if he does die, you have tried your best to keep him..."

Just as Hans was about to finish, he was interrupted by a sound, and, miraculously, Frank turned over and opened his eyes. Hans stunned, stood in place, his mouth wide open. As Hans stood there, the doctor ran over to Frank and checked his blood pressure and pulse.

"Will I be okay?" Frank asked weakly.

"Yes, but part of your colon had to be removed," the doctor said, "You will recover quickly, though."

"How long until he will be able to fight again?" Hans asked.

"It will be about one and a half weeks to two weeks, so it shouldn't be too long."

"That's good because I would hate to disappoint the Kaiser," admitted Frank.

“And I will not fight without a whole crew,” exclaimed Hans.

Frank described what he had experienced, and after that discussion, it was time to eat again. After they finished eating, they were in sight of Zeebrugge. “Land ho!” Hans exclaimed, running into Franks’ room.

“We are already in Germany?” asked Frank.

“No, we are going to Zeebrugge, which is in Belgium,” Hans informed.

“What do you mean? Why are we going to Zeebrugge?” Frank asked.

“I forgot that you were in a coma this whole time. When the destroyer got to the HMS Snow, it used up a lot of fuel to get there, and if we headed back to the Fatherland, we would never make it,” replied Hans.

“That makes sense,” Frank said. Hans said goodbye to Frank and went to the front deck to see Zeebrugge. It had a large number of docks, most of them with destroyers docked beside them. The strange thing was that Germany had only occupied Belgium for a month now, but even the submarine pen was bustling with German subs. Hans could hardly believe he was in Belgium, or that Germany had so completely taken over this quaint little country. It seemed cruel, almost evil, but on the other hand, Germany only wanted to attack France, but Belgium refused to let the German troops simply pass through the country. Only then did the Germans turn to force. He didn’t understand why the press made Germany look like they were cruel and evil animals, and the 'bad' guys. They joined the war to help Austria-Hungary fight against Serbia, who assassinated two very important people, causing turmoil. Nobody thought that Serbia was at fault. Hans thought hard about this as the destroyer docked. Hans limped over to the side of the destroyer and jumped over the side, landing on the dock, pain shot through his limbs and the wounds on his back as he did this, but he didn't care. He never wanted to be on a ship again. The torture he and his crew went through on the HMS Snow was still fresh in his mind. He noticed the name of the destroyer while he waited for the rest of his crew. It was the SMS V191. Once the crew was on the dock, a Gefreiter escorted them to a building behind the submarine pen. There they got new uniforms and pickelhaubes and received treatment for their smaller wounds, such as cuts and bruises. They were served German pot roast and asparagus with pear Schnapps. After the crew had dinner, Hans brought a bowl of potato soup, a slice of Bienenstich, and two bottles of Schnapps to Frank.

"Ah, Schnapps," said Frank, "The nectar of the gods, and even though my favorite flavor is apple, the pear is rather refreshing." Hans sat next to Frank's bed, sipping the other bottle of Schnapps.

"According to another man, we are leaving for the Marne tomorrow afternoon," Hans informed.

"Will I be coming with?" asked Frank.

Hans took a large gulp of Schnapps before replying,

"Yes, you will be coming with, but you are prohibited

from fighting for at least a week and a half, doctor's orders."

"That's insane. I could fight now if I wan-Ah!" Frank sat up too quickly and winced in pain.

Hans pointed at him, "You are only making your case worse. That is why you are barred from combat."

Frank sighed, knowing he could no longer argue.

Hans took one last sip of his Schnapps before saying, "I must leave now; I have work to do. Get better soon." Hans got up, left the room, and walked back to the destroyer. The A7V had been put on the concrete a foot from the dock. It was badly damaged. At least half of the outside of the tank was torn off. A machine gun was, riddled with dents and bullets, but it could be fixed.

Hans went to the sleeping quarters, and, after everything he had been through, fell asleep in seconds. He needed the rest. The next day would be eventful.

Chapter 9
Back to the Marne

Hans stood by a shoddy wall and glanced to his right. The people there were dressed in royal garb. Out of the corner of his eye, he saw people with guns pointed toward them. He looked over his shoulder and saw a man with a gun pointed at him.

"Turn around!" the man demanded in Russian.

Hans somehow understood and turned around.

The last thing he heard was BAM.

Hans woke up with a start, covered in sweat.

It was all a dream, he thought, *but it felt so vivid, almost real. How could I understand Russian? Who were the people next to me, and why were they dressed like royalty?* He had to let his questions go as he suddenly remembered that today they would be returning to the Marne. However, he already knew that he and his crew would not be fighting in the tank. He was happy but also a little disappointed about not being able to use the big gun; however, the good thing was that he wouldn't be so hot and uncomfortable in that big metal machine they called a tank. For breakfast, the crew had some bread and one last bottle of Schnapps. They departed on a threehour train ride to the Marne. Once they arrived, they unloaded all of their gear and were put to work digging trenches with their spades.

"It is so hot out here digging these trenches," Hans complained.

"I know. It's almost like we're POWs. We work ourselves to death just to put money in our wallets and food in our bellies," Fritz replied. The ground was muddy and wet, making for very unpleasant conditions.

The only reason the French machine guns hadn't obliterated them was the fact that they dug the trench on the side of a hill. Digging a trench within range of those machine guns without cover in the afternoon would be suicide. They were digging a supply trench to allow the Germans to push up the lines. Without supplies, those soldiers would be as good as dead. This supply trench was not only crucial for an attack, but it would also play a vital part in defending the area from any counterattack. However, since the crew was digging the trench in the hot sun, they couldn't help complaining.

"Why do we have to dig this?" Fritz grumbled. "We have gone through more in a week than most people have gone through in their entire lives. I have a beautiful wife in Cologne. We want to have a family when this war is over. I would give anything to see her again. Instead, they force us to continue fighting after the hell we've gone through."

"I used to have a wife. Her name was Alice. She had enchanting blue eyes and beautiful blonde hair. But then one day, she contracted Typhoid Fever, and despite all of my prayers, she died. I lost everything I loved; my best friend, my mother, who disowned me, my father, my wife, and the child she would have had if she wouldn't have died. The death of my best friend to a British ladder was the final straw. I joined this war to show the British what they've created— a killing machine bent on revenge," Hans confessed. Those strong words sunk into the crew. They complained about not being able to see their wives, and Hans had lost everything. He had so much anger and sadness, but he kept it to himself, and it was taking a toll on him. Hans knew it would be hard to tell the crew about it, but he also knew that if he hadn't told them, it would have driven him insane. It was almost psychologically impossible to keep that amount of pain inside. It would cause depression, then anger issues, and then eventually suicide or psychosis. The crew knew this as well. They were glad Hans opened up.

The sun had started its trek down the sky, and they were nearly finished digging the trench. When night came, they connected their channel to the long German one that stretched as far as the eye could see. They carried heavy supplies. Two MG08s were set up at the front of the trench. Barbed wire was rolled out near no man's land. By the time the sun peeked out from the horizon, they had created a fully functional trench. Little did they know, their supply trench was about to be tested. As the sun rose in the sky, Hans was eating a can of salted beef, when he heard a whistle. At first, he thought it was a German whistle, and he looked for charging Germans. But, he saw something out of the corner of his eye that didn't seem right, French soldiers. They were charging through no-man's-land.

Hans shouted to his sleeping comrades, "WE'RE UNDER ATTACK," and jumped to a machine gun. Fritz joined him at the other machine gun, mercilessly pumping lead into the charging French. Still, the French continued to advance. The first of them made it to the barbed wire. One of them, stuck on the barbed wire, screamed as the sharp metal barbs dug into his skin. Nobody even bothered to shoot him. They all knew his fate, and so did he. Suddenly, a shot rang out. The man had been shot in the head. Smoke curled from Hans's PO8. He put the man out of his misery because nobody deserved to suffer as he did. He then put his gun into its holster and continued to fire the machine gun. To save himself from immense guilt, he simply thought of the people he was killing as objects that he had to hit with his machine gun. Soon, however, the French began to overwhelm the defending Germans. There were simply too many of them, and snipers slowly picked off the machine gunners. Hans was firing the gun when he heard a loud CRACK. Something flew over the top of his head. The sniper's bullet had just missed him. He knew that every second he kept fighting, death crawled closer, waiting to grab him with its bony fingers and drag him to the fires of Hell for his unholy crimes. He had to retreat.

"RETREAT NOW!" yelled Hans, "I'll hold them off." He looked at Wilhelm, and he nodded. Wilhelm yelled orders to the rest of the crew and led them to the reserve trenches while Hans covered their retreat. He sabotaged the machine guns, and as the French infiltrated the trenches, he threw grenades. BAM BAM BAM BAM BAM Bodies flew into the air. He heard screaming as shrapnel tore through their flesh. He looked toward the reserve trench; the crew was almost there. He pulled out his pistol, looked around the corner and fired. A grenade landed in front of him. Most people would have frozen in fear, but Hans did not cower in the face of danger. He immediately grabbed it and threw the grenade back to its thrower. He heard a scream of horror just before the grenade exploded. Hans heard a commotion close by and fired four shots around the corner. He was now out of ammo. A French soldier rounded the corner and raised his trench club. BAM! The man fell to the ground, dead. Hans saw Fritz at the reserve trench, smoke coming from his gun. He had saved his life.

"Come on," Fritz yelled. Hans nodded and ran as fast as he could with the heavy equipment on his back. Gunshots were coming from both sides, but he made it to the reserve trench unscathed. Once there, Hans again joined the fight against the advancing French.

After a few minutes of holding off the advance, a soldier ran up to the group and yelled, "We have orders to retreat to the Aisne River; trenches are being captured all across the board. Ehrhardt EV/4s will be arriving soon." They just had to hold the line. The French charged the trench, their bayonets fixed, and a maniacal look in their eyes. The crew didn't have machine guns, only their rifles. Hans fired his rifle over and over again. Some men fell dead while others were only wounded. Blood stained the battlefield. Screams of pain could be heard on both sides as people were shot in their limbs, breaking their bones and causing almost unbearable pain.

Hans knew that this kind of brutality was never before thought possible. He, along with many others, believed that this sheer destructiveness would convince humanity to end the senseless chaos that is war. However, there would never be an end to human nature and its cruelty. What Hans didn't know, what he couldn't know was, that, if anything, this war sparked a chain of events that only increased that destruction and terror. With the fall of empires came the rise of dictators who, in the case of Mao Zedong and Joseph Stalin, starved their people, causing even more death. From the cruelty of dictatorships came democracies and civil wars in some countries, and the rise of Communism in others. It sparked even more war, and to this day, battles are still raging around the world. The battle at the Marne was only the beginning.

Hans saw all of the corpses, and, as he fired his rifle, a silent tear rolled down his weathered cheek. He knew that when this terrible war was over, no matter how much they wanted to forget, war veterans would never be able to destroy a memory this traumatic.

Hans knew that even when all the veterans were long dead, stories of the war would be passed on. Even if one day the war was forgotten, there would always be scars, if not on the people, then on the land and the soil. When that day came, the suffering and death will no longer be sad. But, for Hans, what would be sad is the fact that it was forgotten. No WW1 veterans are alive today, but we forgot the war before they were all dead. They watched as we ignored them for politics and new technology. Some, like Hans, died thinking they would be remembered, and they weren't completely naive to think so. It seemed logical to them that it wouldn't be difficult to remember the horrors they had to go through. Others died knowing they would be forgotten. They corrupted their lives and their minds to fight for what they had to, their family. Then they watched the world turn its back on them for an easier to understand, black and white war that wouldn't exist without the Great War. That war was WW2. Millions of lives were senselessly wasted. There isn't any way to sugarcoat it, we forgot. Despite the fact that the Great War was the most significant in history in terms of technological warfare as well as medical advances, we just forgot. Even schools focus heavily on WW2 because more died, and there is a clear start and finish to that war. There is an obvious 'good' and 'bad' side. We even forgot the terrible pandemic that would follow this war. The 1918 Flu pandemic infected every human-inhabited country except for American Samoa. Some estimates suggest it infected 500 million people, one-third of the human population at the time, and killed more than both world wars combined. In fact, some even call it the Forgotten Plague. It ended the war quicker, and the war helped it spread.

Hans would meet H1N1 in his lifetime, but not now.

Right now, he just had to hold the trench for a few more minutes. The advance was beginning to weaken, mainly because many of the French were dead. Hans just kept firing, only stopping to reload. There were so many corpses. So many people had fallen at the hands of Hans Fitzgerald. He had been wounded so many times, yet he refused to die. He would lay down his life before he let the French hurt his comrades and the country he was born and raised in. Yet he was also very obedient. He would only retreat if he was ordered to do so. Soon he heard the sound of the Ehrhardts approaching the trench. He was able to get a quick glance at the rustic vehicles. They were dark gray, and they looked like standard cars, except for the fact that they were covered in armored plating. They also had a turret on the top with an iron cross on it, and a machine gun in the front. They were incredibly intimidating steel monsters. As he looked back once more, he saw a man gesturing to come to the vehicle he was near. Hans nodded and quickly ran to the car. Bullets flew past him as he left the safety of the trench.

Many of the fleeing Germans did not survive the retreat. Herman was shot in his ulna, shattering it. However, Hans safely made it to the vehicle. Fritz was shot in his adductor magnus and his deltoid, but he too made it to safety.

Hans opened the hatch to the vehicle and climbed inside. He ran to a machine gun on the side of the car. French soldiers ran toward the vehicles. He fired the machine gun. RAT TAT TAT TAT. French soldiers fell. RAT TAT TAT TAT. More. RAT TAT TAT TAT. More. He tried to fight back, but the gun had limited space to fire, and he couldn't even see the left part of the vehicle from his small visor. He heard French soldiers firing at the vehicles with their rifles. Some even threw grenades, which caused substantial damage to the lightly armored cars.

Hans yelled to the driver, "Drive! Drive now!" After getting no response, he decided to investigate. The driver lay dead, shot in the head by a sniper. In the chaos of telling everyone to get to the vehicle, he had made himself an easy target for the French snipers. Hans looked out of the hatch and saw wounded soldiers running to the vehicle. Only four of them made it. One manned the turret. Two of the other soldiers tended to a heavily wounded soldier, whom they had helped into the car. Hans took the throttle and gave it some gas.

Chapter 10
The Aisne River

The Ehrhardt lurched and began to drive away. Hans had no idea how to get to the Aisne River. He would have to guess or follow the other vehicles. Three other vehicles drove in front of him, and he followed close behind. After driving for five minutes, he heard engines on the left and right side of him.

"Look at our flanks! I hear something," Hans yelled to the man in the turret,

The man looked, his eyes widened in fear, and he yelled back to Hans, "They're French War Cars!" The vehicles fired machine guns loaded with anti-tank shells at the Ehrhardt. The bullets easily pierced the thin armor. At this rate, it would be torn to bits. Hans had an idea.

"Hey, you, take the wheel," he yelled to the man in the turret. At once, the man climbed out of the turret and into the driver's position.

Hans went to the turret, "Ram against the vehicle on the right. Try and run it off the road," he ordered. Hans tried to fire at the War Car, but the turret received a hail of anti-tank bullets, disabling it. They hit the car, trying to destroy it. The vehicle refused to let up its relentless assault. It was time for plan B. Hans opened the hatch of the turret, and climbed on top of the Ehrhardt. The fierce wind threatened to tear him off the vehicle. He slowly stood up and then jumped onto the War Car. A French soldier stared at Hans in complete surprise, before Hans punched him in the face, knocking him off the car. Another man aimed his rifle at Hans. Hans grabbed the barrel of the gun with both hands, yanked it out of the man's arms, and slammed him in the head with the stock, knocking him unconscious. The gunner turned the machine gun toward him, and Hans shot him in the chest. Another man tried to stab Hans with a knife. Hans blocked the blow with the rifle, dropping it and sending the man off the side of the car with an uppercut.

Lastly, Hans punched the driver out of his seat and took the wheel. He drove around the back of the Ehrhardt and approached the other War Car. He put ammo packs on the gas pedal to keep it at a steady speed and raced to the anti-tank machine gun. He quickly demolished the other car. The vehicle exploded, but then it swerved right into Hans's car. Thrown to the ground, Hans bounced on the path, sharp rocks digging into his skin. Entire sheets of skin were torn from his body. Once he came to a stop, he laid there, trying to comprehend what had happened. He was in France, in enemy territory, in the middle of nowhere. He suddenly felt pain in his right arm, and he lifted it.

It was dislocated. Blood oozed everywhere due to multiple abrasions. He struggled to stand and survey his surroundings. There were many farms, with a few patches of woodland. In the distance, he saw a town. He picked up his now dented pickelhaube, which provided no protection whatsoever, but to him, it symbolized everything he was fighting for— his crew and his country. He looked at an area of woodland and knew that it would provide him protection as well as sustenance for his journey. As he started toward the forest, he realized how injured he was. He had lost his medical kit in all of the chaos that had ensued; therefore, he had no painkillers for his arm. It hurt so badly his eyes watered. He almost lost consciousness from the pain.

Must…keep…going...must...keep...going, he silently chanted. But, his body couldn't take any more suffering, and he collapsed. He came to moments later and staggered into the forest. He dropped to the soil and leaned against a rock. Hans took off his uniform and inspected the damage. His left pectoral muscle was badly bruised, and he was sure he had broken two ribs. All of the skin was ripped off his right shoulder, revealing his bone. His handsome and muscular body was nearly destroyed. He put his uniform back on and walked around the forest, scrounging for berries. He soon found some green ones. Hans was desperate and ate a few, before beginning his journey. He walked for about 15 minutes before his stomach cramped. He doubled over in pain. Hans barely got his pants down before diarrhea hit. The cramping was unbearable. Only then did he remember the last thing he ate, the green berries. Hans had eaten buckthorn berries, and while they wouldn't kill him, they would cause suffering. He staggered through the field, carrying his pants. There was no way he could put them back on now. He was close to the town and figured he could find a place to stay. A mild concussion kept him from thinking clearly, and he walked through the town half-naked. He was near a small house when a French woman walked out of the door. She was about to take an evening walk when she saw Hans.

"Oh my," she said. Hans caught her staring at his groin, and he quickly concealed it with his hand.

"I...I was just looking for a place to stay the night," Hans said in French, blushing and feeling very self-conscious.

"You can stay the night with me," the young woman said flirtatiously and smiled at him. Hans thought about running, but after she gave him another dazzling smile, he decided against his better judgment and walked into the house.

"Why are you limping? Let me take a look," she said.

"Uh...no, it's nothing," Hans said sheepishly.

"Come in the bedroom, and I'll take a look," she said and walked him into the room. At first, Hans resisted, but after she kissed him, he lay down on the bed. So she took off his shirt and looked at all of his injuries.

"I'll take care of you," she said. Hans was incredibly uncomfortable at the moment. She ran her hand down his chest and abdomen, and that, for him, was crossing the line.

"Stop, I'm not that kind of guy. Just treat my wounds," Hans growled. The woman rolled her eyes and grabbed some gauze. She knew what she was doing as she expertly wrapped it around his wounds and then, with a little effort, pushed his arm back into its socket.

She stared at him.

After two minutes of her intense staring, Hans finally gave in, "Fine. Kiss me woman," he whispered. She nodded and turned off the lamp. Hans had the best night he'd had in years.

He woke up at 8:00 a.m., still in bed with the French woman. She was staring at him, rubbing his neck. "You sure know how to show a woman a good time. Have you thought of a name for our child?" she asked. Hans's eyes widened, and he asked, "Our what?" She looked at him strangely before saying, "Our child." Hans gasped. He quickly jumped out of the bed, grabbed his clothes, and ran. Once outside, he got dressed and ran out of the town. He looked back and saw a sign declaring the town's name. *La Chaussée*. Hans ran to the river before slowing and walking along the riverbank. *Should I have done that*? Hans wondered. *What would Alice say if she was alive, and she found out that I had done that with another woman*? He struggled with doubt and self scorn, and soon, his head and his heart were in an intense argument. *You only did it because you're a widower, not because you loved her more than Alice*.

Hans's mind struggled with his love for Alice, his faith, and his belief in the teachings of the Bible against the urges and desires he'd held at bay for so long since losing his wife. Nearly dying every day, and suffering through torture and constant attacks had taken a toll on him that one night with a woman did a lot to repair. For the first time in a long time, he felt like a man again and not just a soldier. Hans walked along the river, easing his feelings of guilt by enjoying nature. France was quite beautiful, at least everything other than the trenches. He even thought about turning around and starting a new life with the woman, walking away from the horrors of war, and settling down to the life he'd always wanted. But, then he remembered his comrades, who were most likely in great danger, if not dead already. He made up his mind right then. When the Great War ended, he would return to La Chaussée and start a family. If he survived, that is. After walking all day along the river, he decided to try and catch a fish. He took a long stick and started walking. He saw a zander by the shallow part of the Marne. Hans used the stick to break its back. He pulled the floating fish out of the water, laid it on the shore, and made a fire to cook it. He ate everything except the bones and fell asleep. When he woke up about two hours later, he began walking again. He found another town, but before he approached it, he rendered a farmer unconscious and stole his clothes. When he got into town, he walked to a market and approached a lady looking at goods.

"Hey, handsome, what can I do for you?" she asked.

"I need directions to the Aisne River. I have a brother there, and I want to give him a gift," Hans answered.

"I can drive you there if you'd like. A good-looking guy like you is the type of person I like to help out," she replied, flirting.

Hans accepted and sat next to her in her car.

"There is a small price, though," she said.

"And what is that?" Hans asked.

"Give me the best kiss you can," she answered. Hans prepared himself and gave her a long romantic kiss on the lips. Suddenly, she fainted. He sat back in horror, stared at her pretty face, and wondered what to do. . She came to after a few minutes.

"Oh, thank you," she said, and gave Hans a hug. "My emotions have been under great strain as my husband died yesterday while pushing the Huns back from the Marne. They found the wreckage of the vehicle he was driving. They think he broke his neck after a Hun hijacked his vehicle and threw him out of the car. Those damn Huns, taking him away like that. You just reminded me that there will always be other men to love." Hans nodded, choosing not to tell her that it was he who killed her husband. She turned to the wheel and stepped on the gas pedal. After driving for an hour in silence, they reached the Aisne River.

"There you are, sir, the Aisne River, I hope your brother enjoys his gift." Hans nodded and climbed out of the car. It was dark out, but he could see the quaint houses lining the banks of the river. On the other side of the river, he could see Germans holding oil lamps while other soldiers dug new trenches. Hans waved goodbye to the lady, waited for her to leave, and then approached the Aisne. It looked to be approximately 30 meters wide.

He quickly swam across the river, and when the Germans pointed guns at him, he simply said, "Guten abend, freunde," and saluted. He explained to them why he was wearing the clothes of a farmer and why he came from the other side of the Aisne. After he told them the story, he walked over to a command tent, where he found Wilhelm talking to Alexander von Kluck, commander of the German 1st Armee. Hans asked him where to find the crew.

"Frank, Herman, and Fritz are in the medical tent," Wilhelm replied. Hans walked to the medical tent and embraced all of his friends. After everything they had been through, they were more than just a crew. They were a family. They were brothers. Now, after losing everything, he had a family once again. This war tore humanity apart, but in an odd way, it also brought humanity together. *After all, you get closest to the people who have gone with you to Hell and back*, Hans thought. *In essence, that's what true war was, a living hell. This war changed combat forever. Just a few years prior, they fought by standing in lines, almost politely. By the time this war was over, there were calculated strategies, tanks, warships, gas, and deadliest of all, artillery*, Hans realized as he looked into the tired eyes of his new family.

"What happened to you?" Herman asked.

Hans told them about his journey from the Marne to La Chaussée to another town to the Aisne. He also told them that he honed in certain *skills* during the journey. Fritz laughed, gave him a mischievous smile, and told him that he had plans to do the same with a nurse when everyone had gone to sleep. In a few minutes, the nurse came to check on Fritz. He whispered into her ear, and she nodded and giggled.

When she left, he said, "I can be very charming when I want to be." Hans smiled, shook his head, and went into a tent filled with beds. He was asleep as soon as his head hit the pillow.

Hans woke in the medical bed, looked to his right and saw a dying soldier. He was turning blue, and his nose was bleeding. His bed was brown from severe diarrhea. Hans then looked to his left and saw doctors cutting a man's chest open. A frothy and bloody substance poured out of the man's lungs. Hans also had a bloody nose, and he couldn't breathe. A nurse tried to comfort him as he waited for the doctors. Hans looked behind her and saw blue corpses stacked against the wall, bleeding out of their orifices. Bodies were on the floor too, and suddenly, a doctor near him collapsed. Another doctor walked over to him, felt his forehead, then dragged him over and dropped him on the pile of corpses. There was no room for the sick or the dead. The other doctors finally finished working on the man to his left, and walked over to Hans. He saw a nurse push the man on the right off the bed. He was as good as dead. Hans feverishly looked at the doctors as they cut his chest open. Frothy liquid poured out. He started to breathe once again. Then the fever overtook him, and he too was pushed to the floor, left to die.

Hans sat up on the bed, soaked in sweat. This dream had been even more vivid than the last. In the dream, it felt like he was actually dying.

What illness could kill so many? It was like influenza. But influenza is not that deadly. The symptoms were very strange. It was like an epidemic. Hans got up and went into the medical tent. He found a doctor tending to some of the patients.

"Do you have a book about all recorded epidemics?" Hans asked.

"Yes, over by my bookshelf," the doctor answered. After looking, Hans found the book. He looked at all the epidemics, and couldn't find the culprit. The closest he found was the Russian Flu. However, the symptoms were not as severe as in his dream.

Hans told the doctor his dream, and when he finished, the doctor said, "That would be unlikely. Many experts believe we'll have eradicated illnesses in just a few years. It was just a dream, anyway." Hans shrugged, walked back into the room, and went back to bed.

In the morning, Hans took a walk by the newly dug trenches. Suddenly, he saw a French soldier running toward the river. Hans ran to a supply tent, grabbed a rifle, and shot the man. The man continued to run. Hans fired again, no response. Then something very strange happened. The man ran across the Aisne. As the man neared, he looked almost transparent. A soldier ran beside Hans, swearing at him for shooting at nothing. The translucent soldier charged at the two of them, his bayonet fixed. Suddenly, the figure charged through the other man and disappeared. The man next to Hans started spasming as if having a seizure. He fell to the ground, screaming and writhing until he was still. Hans yelled for a doctor, who ran to the man and checked his pulse.

"This man is dead," the doctor gravely informed him. However, as the doctor looked at the body, he saw no wounds whatsoever.

As soldiers ran out to see the body, they yelled at Hans, "You murdered Charles, you bastard."

"No. I promise I didn't. It looked like he had a seizure before he died." Hans yelled.

Suddenly, a man yelled out, "This man is innocent, and I can prove it." A young soldier walked to the body.

He yelled to the crowd, "I was a priest before this war, and I can sense a presence within this dead man. He took out a cross. As he put it close to the corpse, the skin began to sizzle. It then started to burn. He took holy water and poured it on the body. Just before the water touched the corpse, it turned into blood.

The man turned to the dumbstruck crowd, "This is an act of evil spirits, not this man. Only evil spirits are harmed by the cross. We can only give him a proper burial after I have finished an exorcism to banish the demons back to Hell." After he said this, many of the soldiers refused to believe him, but others quickly said a prayer with fear in their eyes. Many of them had been Christians before the war, and they feared evil spirits, for they knew nobody was safe from demonic possession. Even hours after the incident, some of the soldiers looked at Hans accusingly. Once during lunch, a soldier ran at Hans and punched him in the face. The man was yelling at Hans, tears in his eyes. Hans stood up, mouth bleeding, and walked up to the man. Hans's eyes were full of sadness, and he embraced the man.

"I did not kill that man. You know as well as I do that nobody here would ever waste precious ammo on nothing. I am sorry he is dead, but he had no wounds. Had I poisoned him, he would have died during the night. My only explanation is that something supernatural happened this morning. I saw a soldier. He was transparent and ran on top of the Aisne. He killed Charles. You don't need to believe me, but I promise I did not kill him," Hans said softly. The man looked at him and nodded in gratitude. He walked away, leaving Hans to finish his lunch. After lunch, Hans walked to the command tent and asked General Kluck if the defenses were all ready.

"Yes. The artillery has just arrived. Those French bastards will find out just how strong Germany really is. I suspect we will crush them and take Paris in a few weeks at most. We must not disappoint the Kaiser," Kluck replied.

"If Germany is as powerful as you say, what happened at the Marne?" Hans asked.

"The biggest problem was lack of supplies. Our army had already taken so much ground. The advance on Paris was too much. Now, we have everything we need to capture France. Now run along Gefreiter Fitzgerald, a good soldier like you always has work to do. Just remember that I have heard of your heroism, but don't get cocky. That's what defeats the best of us," Kluck answered.

Hans decided to take a look at the new artillery pieces. When he saw them, he couldn't believe his eyes. They were so beautiful, despite being caked with mud. Every mechanical detail was perfect. They almost looked like a special type of creature. They were howitzers, much like the turret on the crew's A7V. However, these were smaller, and when Hans looked at the side of them, they were all labeled sFH 13. As he looked at the artillery, he saw large vehicles driving towards the camp in the distance. At first, Hans didn't recognize it. It looked like a large metal box with a turret on top. As it neared, Hans noticed some of the smaller dents, and he suddenly knew what it was.

"The A7V," he yelled to the camp, "It's back." Wilhelm came running to the artillery and saw their beloved tank.

"It's beautiful," he muttered. He wasn't kidding. It had gotten new camo and it wasn't torn apart or smoking anymore. It had the same personality, but it was no longer dying. It was reborn. Once the vehicle arrived, a soldier hopped out.

"Is one of you Fritz Fischer?" he asked. "He is the driver of this tank." Hans yelled for Fritz. After about a minute, Fritz stumbled out of the medical tent, his eyes sparkling. He smiled at their tank.

Fritz turned toward the soldier, "Yes, I am Fritz Fischer." The man nodded and walked to the command tent.

"She is gorgeous," Fritz said, "a work of art." He now had a new engine to drive. The damaged engine had forced Fritz to expend huge amounts of strength to control the dying beast. Hans then ran all around the camp, looking for the rest of the crew. After five minutes, he had gathered them all. When they saw the tank, they cheered. They had all had enough of the trenches. In the tank, they were immune to bullets, grenades, shrapnel, fire, and even other tanks to a certain extent. At times it was the only thing that stood between them and death. After gazing at it a bit longer, Hans walked back to the newly-dug trenches with his crew. They played Mensch ärgere Dich nicht. Wilhelm was winning, when Hans suddenly put his playing piece on top of Wilhelm's and moved it to his 'out' area. Wilhelm cursed, and everyone else laughed and commented. After the horrors they had witnessed, they could finally laugh and have fun again. They played long after the sun had dipped below the horizon. The war was forgotten. They felt at home. In the end, they didn't care who won the game. To them, all they needed was each other, and tomorrow, they would need each other more than ever.

Chapter 11

The Trenches and the Tanks

Hans woke up in the trench. A rat crawled up his uniform, and he swatted it. It squeaked and scampered away. The rest of the crew was also sleeping, except for Fritz. A sliver of the sun peeked above the horizon. They had fallen asleep while playing the game. Hans remembered how much he had enjoyed it. He knew they would not find another time to relax like that for a while. After stretching, Hans stood up. He noticed movement out of the corner of his eye. He looked over the Aisne and saw what it was. Trenches. The French had dug trenches during the night. Hans hurriedly climbed out of the trench and ran into the command tent. He ran to Kluck, who was looking at a map sleepily.

"The French have dug trenches overnight. We need to prepare for an attack," Hans yelled at the general.

"Sound the alarm," Kluck gravely said. Hans ran to the sleeping quarters and sounded the crude alarm.

"Get up! The French are here!" Hans yelled as loud as he could. In just a few minutes, the entire camp was ready to defend an attack. Soldiers manned the artillery. Snipers lined the trenches. They set up 17-centimeter Minenwerfers behind the camp. Machine gunners loaded the guns, waiting patiently. Kluck yelled orders to everyone, keeping everyone working. Everyone had a job. Hans was assigned to the turret of the tank once again. He noticed that a shell was already loaded into the barrel. They just had to wait. After about half an hour, Hans was getting impatient. But then he heard the whistle blow and tanks emerged from the woodland. They were crude but dangerous. Anti-tank machine guns lined the tanks. However, they were much smaller than the A7V. Hans aimed at one of the leading tanks and fired. The huge shell easily pierced its thick armor. It flew high into the sky, fire everywhere. The burnt metal rained down upon the enemy. An unlucky man was pinned to the ground by a large piece of molten shrapnel. The fire quickly devoured him. Another piece of shrapnel collided with a tank, rendering it useless. Hans reloaded the gun and fired once again. Another tank exploded. The battle was deafening. There was even more blood than at the Marne. The banks of the Aisne were soaked in the blood of soldiers. Some soldiers attempted to swim across the river, only to be killed before reaching the shore. An enemy tank fired at the A7V. Hans heard screams and destroyed it quickly. Once again, their tank was being ripped apart, piece by piece. And then, the engine was silent.

"What's going on down there?" Hans yelled down to Fritz.

"I don't know. I'll go check it out," Fritz yelled back. Anti-tank bullets tore through the turret, nearly killing Hans. He continued to fire at the tanks. One by one, they flew into the sky in huge explosions. There was only one left. The final tank targeted the turret; it was the true anti-tank threat. Hans saw blood, but kept looking for the tank. He couldn't feel his body. Everything was numb and cold, or possibly hot, he couldn't tell. There. Hans finally spotted the tank and fired. Success. The last tank was gone.

Light mortars lined the French trenches, targeting the tank. Some of the shells caused deep dents, while others barely punctured it. Hans aimed at the trenches. Vast parts of the trenches exploded. Some soldiers suffocated under the dirt, having been paralyzed or fatally wounded. Gradually, after firing shell after shell at the trenches, the mortar fire began to dissipate. They were holding the line. During the battle, Hans learned an important lesson: the use of large armies wins the battle, but the use of terrain wins the war. The French had gained no ground the entire time; they simply couldn't cross the river without being exposed. The Aisne was at least 12 feet deep, making it impossible for anything to cross. For the next half hour, they attacked to no avail. Thousands lay on the wretched battlefield, dead for nothing—so much senseless death. The Germans, however, had died for a better reason—stopping the French at the Aisne, perhaps saving many from death. The soldiers were oblivious to the fact that they had just started trench warfare. As the sun sat in the sky at noon, watching the battle in disappointment of humanity, Hans fired his final shell, and then there was silence. They had done it. The French had exhausted their army. Germany reigned supreme. Hans cheered at the realization and went to the base of the tank. The rest of the crew was not cheering. They were kneeling by something. Hans saw what they were looking at and felt sick to his stomach. Heinrich lay on the ground, covered in blood, unmoving. He was dead. Hans ran out of the tank, nearly crying, and vomited. Then he noticed something. Blood. Lots of it. This time, he had not escaped injury. He was riddled with bullet holes. He felt a wave of nausea, and fell forward into the blood and vomit soaked mud.

Hans was lying in a bed but felt no pain. Doctors surrounded him. He felt nauseous and groggy. He wasn't bleeding any more. He was nearly naked. He counted seven bullet holes across his body. As pain returned to his body, he tried to speak but couldn't hear his voice, as if he was in a dream. A doctor nodded and took out a needle filled with liquid. He injected the needle into Hans's arm. Hans shuddered, but the pain soon subsided. He felt greatly relieved as his muscles relaxed. The doctors began sewing the wounds together except for one—the one on his chest. It was his lung. He had been shot in the lung. During the battle, due to adrenaline, Hans had not even noticed that it was hard to breathe, and he had been coughing up blood.

They were cutting the wound open now. The doctors conversed, before one of them took out another needle. They put it into his arm. Almost immediately, Hans fell asleep.

When he woke, the wound was stitched back together. Once again, he was groggy.

"Will I live?" Hans asked the doctors near him. "Yes, though you have a long road to recovery. You broke 18 bones, and we had to remove your left lung," one of the doctors replied. Hans nodded. He thanked the doctors for saving his life. He was amazed that he could breathe normally, having only one lung. He looked around, and knew he would be there for a long time. Hans called for Wilhelm, who quickly came.

"What did you do with him?" Hans asked.

"We will bury him by the fields," Wilhelm answered sadly. "He deserves to be buried somewhere peaceful. This was his pickelhaube." Wilhelm showed it to Hans. It had a large bullet hole right through the head of the German eagle. As Hans looked at the pickelhaube, he remembered what Heinrich had done. He had saved the tank in Paris, willing to sacrifice his life for the crew. He had been one of the gunners, defending Germany from the French beast. He remembered the night before when they had played Mensch ärgere Dich nicht together. They were all so happy. Now, Heinrich was dead. But he had died a good man, fighting until he could fight no more. He would be remembered.

Hans struggled to hold back tears. Wilhelm decided to give him some time alone, and went to bury Heinrich.

Days after that, the entire crew grieved Heinrich. Wilhelm came every day to talk to Hans, Fritz, Herman, and Frank in their beds. After two weeks passed, Frank left the medical tent, once again ready to fight. Wilhelm informed them that they had been holding off the French successfully. In October, Wilhelm told Hans that the Ottoman Empire had joined the war. After another month, Hans finally left the hospital tent. The first thing he did was walk to the field behind the battlefield. He saw the cross and the pickelhaube resting on it. Grass had grown over the grave, and Hans remembered the months before. Wilted poppies sat around the gravesite. Hans kneeled at the cross and paid his respects. After a few minutes, Wilhelm appeared.

He put his hand on Hans's shoulder and said, "Hans, you need to move on. Heinrich is dead, let it go. It's what he would have wanted."

Hans looked at the grave one last time before saying, "You're right. Come on. We've got a war to win."

Chapter 12
Ypres

Hans was in another Ehrhardt. He shuddered at the thought of the last time he had been in one. The rest of the crew was also there. They were heading to a place called Ypres. For the last few days, a battle had been raging there. They were almost there. Hans thought it was strange that the fighting kept going north. Ypres was in Belgium. He began to see craters in the ground– a lot of them. The French had hammered the city with artillery. Suddenly, there it was. Ypres. Hans noticed the new trenches first and then the bitter fighting. There were no vehicles—just soldiers. The sky was cloudy, and it started to rain. It was a terrible November day. The Ehrhardt stopped. All the soldiers exited the vehicle. They ran to the trenches as fast as they could. Hans quickly took out his rifle and fired at the trenches. He missed his target. He fired shot after shot before he heard the whistle.

An officer yelled, "Over the top!" Hans remembered the last time he had been over the top. He leaped over the trench and charged, bayonet fixed. The French fired their machine guns at them. Soldiers fell all around him. He quickly dived into a crater. He looked up and saw something in the sky. Shells. They were heading down toward the Germans. The other Germans began to retreat. Hans was about to as well, but the shells landed. BOOM. BOOM. BABOOM. BOOM. Hans was thrown forward, landing in the dirt. He got up and realized he was right in front of the French trench. He leaped into it and took out his Nahkampfmesser knife. Smoke was everywhere. He heard sounds coming from the German lines. It was the troops. They were using the smoke to hide their exact positions. Hans heard the French guns firing, and knew his duty. He slithered through the trenches and found the first machine gunner. He went up behind the soldier, put the knife in front of the man, and thrust it into the man's left eye. The knife went into his brain, killing him instantly. The soldiers were so busy fighting that they didn't realize the real enemy was walking amongst them. As Hans was about to kill the next man, he missed his eye. The blade glanced off the cartilage on his nose. The man turned around and punched Hans. Hans stumbled to the back of the trench. He leaped towards the man and pushed him in front of his own machine gun. Hans fired the machine gun and blew the man's face open. Some of the other French soldiers noticed the commotion and were about to shoot Hans. Just before they could fire, the Germans assaulted the trench. Bullets flew everywhere. Hans grabbed a rifle from a dead soldier. He thrust the bayonet into a soldier's gut. He felt a strange sense of déjà vu. He then saw more French soldiers coming from their nearby communication trench. Hans knew they couldn't hold this trench much longer. Suddenly, a new German soldier jumped into the trench. He had a gas mask and a large metal tank on his back. He was holding what appeared to be a hose. He pushed past everyone. The enemy fired at him, but the shots bounced off. Suddenly, flames shot out the nozzle of the hose. Hans remembered the weapon. A flamethrower. The flames devoured the flesh of the enemy. Burning soldiers climbed out of the trench, only to be killed by German machine guns. A horrible smell filled the air, causing many of the soldiers to vomit. Hans caught glimpses of what appeared to be skeletons running through the fire. Finally, the soldier with the flamethrower stopped. The Germans began to advance. Hans saw so many black skeletons on the ground. One corpse leaned on the side of the trench, his face burned beyond recognition. Another body was lying on the ground, only one eye still intact. The soldier walked into the communications tent. The tent caught on fire as he killed the French. Hans wanted to warn the man, but he was too late. The tarp fell. The soldiers watched in horror as the man struggled and screamed under the burning tent before he was still. Now, they were on their own. They moved in on the reserve trench and quickly slaughtered the remaining soldiers. Then, they abandoned the trenches and advanced on the city. Many of the buildings had been reduced to rubble, providing the perfect environment for snipers. As the army marched, men fell one by one. Hans saw a muzzle flash coming from a building, and he fired there. The sniper was silenced. They were in the city. The French continued to harass the troops, slowly weakening them. Then Hans saw it, an armored train sat idly by a train station. It had five planes on it. French soldiers were being evacuated. Hans quickly got the crew, and they walked over to the train. The French soldiers put their hands up. Then they put them down. Hans felt something on his back and turned around. French soldiers surrounded them. When the crew realized their situation, they put their hands up. The soldiers forced them into the train and locked them in a car. After a short time, the train started moving. The crew sat in sad silence for hours, before Hans spoke. "Are we just going to sit here? There must be a way out."

"Hans, just give up. There's no way out. We'll probably die here," Wilhelm answered. But, Hans suddenly had an idea.

"What if one of us pretends to have a heart attack? Maybe we could fool the guards into providing us with an escape." The crew talked and decided it was a good idea.

"I'll do it," said Wilhelm, "I'm the oldest. It would be the most convincing if I did it." The crew agreed and sat against the car. Wilhelm stood up and clutched his chest. His eyes widened. He yelled in pain.

"Oh, my God!" Hans yelled, "He's having a heart attack!" They heard footsteps, and just as Wilhelm fell over, a French soldier unlocked the back door.

"That's too bad," the man said, "more fuel for the engi..."Hans snapped the man's neck, and he fell over, dead. Wilhelm got up, and the crew ran through the back door. In the next car, a man was operating a turret. The crew quietly sneaked past him. They opened the door and found a surprise— the planes. They were strapped down to wooden platforms, but they all knew what to do. Hans and Fritz ran to the first plane, Herman and Frank went to the second plane, and Wilhelm went to the third plane. Hans started the plane and tried to take off. At first, the straps held firm, but they finally broke free. Hans had never flown before, but the controls seemed basic. As the plane flew into the air, Hans realized something. There were no trees anywhere, only sand. They were in the desert. As the plane flew into the air, the arid wind showed no mercy. Hans heard something. TA TA TA TA TA TA TA TA. Hans looked below the plane. The train was attacking. All the turrets were focused on the planes. Hans's plane took heavy fire. The wooden plane shook as the guns tore through it. Hans noticed that under the plane controls, there was a large stock or grenades. These planes were bombers. He turned the nose toward the train.

"What are you doing?" Fritz yelled.

"We got a train to destroy," Hans responded. As he neared the train, he experimented with evading the wrath of the turrets. Then the time came. Hans flew right over the back turret and threw an anti-tank grenade. BOOOOOOM-MMMM. The turret exploded. One down, five to go. Scratch that. More explosions rang out across the desert. The crew had caught on. Hans bombed the front turret, destroying it. BOOM. BOOM. The last two turrets were destroyed, now for the front. Hans flew over the top of the front and threw a grenade. The front of the train blew open. There was just one more thing to do. He flew over the planes strapped to the train and threw an incendiary grenade. The fire burned both planes. Hans cheered, for he had destroyed an armored train. However, he accidentally kicked an incendiary grenade. He tried to snuff out the flames with his boot, but sent an ember into the wing of the plane. The wing burst into flames. The fire ate through the wood. Hans was losing control of the plane as smoke blinded him and Fritz. The entire right part of the aircraft was burning. It started to spiral toward the ground.

"JUMP!" Hans yelled to Fritz. Fritz looked at Hans, his face full of uncertainty before he jumped out of the smoking plane. Hans looked at the desert as it sped toward him, and he too jumped.

Chapter 13
The Ottoman Empire

Hans landed in the sand. While it partially cushioned his fall, the 90-foot drop cracked a few of his ribs. After a few minutes, he managed to collect himself, and he staggered up. He saw the wreckage of the plane, still burning. There was desert as far as the eye could see. Behind him, he saw the two other planes, and the crew talking to each other. Fritz was with them, holding his broken nose. Hans stumbled over to them. They all greeted him, and they embraced each other, happy that they were alive. As Hans took a look at the other planes, he quickly realized a problem. The bottoms of the planes were destroyed.

Wilhelm saw Hans looking at the planes, and said, "Nobody here knew how to fly a plane. It's also nearly impossible to land in the sand without wrecking something." They all looked solemnly at the broken planes, and they all seemed to realize something at the same time.

Hans said it first, "We're in the middle of a scorching desert with no transportation." It was true. They didn't even know what country they were in or which way to go. Hans had an idea.

“What if we followed the train rails? It was obviously heading somewhere.” The crew agreed, and they walked toward the rails. They saw the train they had destroyed. Its armor was demolished. They had slain the British monster. Once they reached the rails, they walked along them. The hot sun plagued them, and there was no shade. The heat was terrible; even the sand scorched their skin. Hans wanted so badly to collapse and try to cool off somehow, but he knew that if he did, it would be the end of him. After walking in the hot sun for about half an hour, Hans, reaped of his energy, saw something— a camp. Though extremely far off, it was a sanctuary. Now, after walking in the desert this long, Hans was no stranger to mirages, but he noticed that the rest of the crew saw it as well. They all staggered as fast as they could to the camp. They were only a few hundred feet away from it. None of them noticed the British flag flying. Finally, they reached it. They walked into the camp and saw a soldier standing on guard.

As they approached him, he said, “what you mates be doin’ wearin’ those uniforms? They what Jerry wears.” The crew looked at each other.

“We are spies. We sneak into German trenches and find their secrets. We were coming here on a train, but the Germans attacked it, and we were the only survivors,” Wilhelm answered. The British soldier nodded, and the crew stared at Wilhelm in disbelief.

"There is one thing, though," the soldier said to Wilhelm, "Why you got Jerry's accent?"

Wilhelm quickly recovered, and said, "We've been sneaking into their trenches for so long now, we developed accents to trick them." The soldier looked content with this answer.

"Do you know where some water is? We've been in the hot sun for so long," Wilhelm asked.

The British soldier burst out in laughter, "Water? Water? You're really that daft? You fink we got fresh water just lyin' around? We're in the desert. We don't have a damn drop to spare. So if you want your *water*, maybe you should take a walk in the bloody desert and find some. Does that sound good?" Wilhelm looked at the man, anger in his eyes. He walked away, and the rest of the crew followed him. They saw that the camp was full of soldiers. They also saw vehicles. There was a D-Type Vauxhall, which meant that there was a high-ranking official at the camp. All they had to do was escape.

Hans whispered to Wilhelm, "When night comes, we can escape camp on the vehicles." They all agreed, and walked to the sleeping quarters. They passed the time by playing cards with some British soldiers. Soon the sun was setting. They went to the mess hall to eat bully beef, bread, and biscuits. After this, they sat with some soldiers and told them about their adventures; they just changed the story a bit to make it sound like they were killing Germans. Now, darkness was upon them, and despite it being scorching in the desert during the day, at night, it was much colder. They all went to the sleeping quarters. They waited until everyone was asleep. Then, one by one, they snuck out. They were divided into three cars. They all looked at each other and said a silent prayer that they would make it out alive. They assumed that friendly soldiers would be far ahead of the camp.

Then, when they were ready, Wilhelm whispered, "Drei, Zwei, Ein." Hans stepped on the gas pedal, and he sped through the camp. A guard ran in front of the vehicle. Hans hit him, and blood splattered the windshield. The car made it out of the camp and was speeding through the sand. He heard gunshots from behind the vehicle, but ignored them. Hans kept his foot on the gas pedal. After a while, there was only silence. The three vehicles drove through the sand, watching for anything on the horizon. Minutes passed. Nothing. Then, they saw trenches on the edge of the horizon. As they neared it, machine guns started to fire at the vehicles.

"Oh my God!" Hans yelled, "They think we're the enemy." The windshield was blown to bits, and glass tore through Hans's uniform. He had no idea what to do. Abandoning the vehicle would be suicide. However, he was afraid he would not make it to the trenches alive if he continued to drive. Then, he thought of something. He ducked below the windshield and put all of his weight on the gas pedal. The bullets bounced off the metal Hans was hiding behind. BAAAM. The front of the vehicle fell into the trench.

Hans was thrown forwards into the metal. It hurt immensely, but he would be fine. He heard the two other cars crash near him. He slowly climbed out of the vehicle. Soldiers were all around the car, their rifles pointed at Hans. He put his hands up.

One of the men asked, "Neden alman üniforması giyiyorsun?" Hans stared at the soldier in confusion.

"What?" Hans asked in German.

"Almanca mı konuşuyorsun?" the soldiers asked. Hans sighed and took something out of his uniform. The iron cross. One of the soldiers nodded his head and ran into an underground dugout. A few seconds later, an older man climbed out.

"Hello, ally," the man said in German. Hans smiled. Then Hans quickly said, "The people in those other vehicles are my friends. Please do not harm them. Who are you people?"

The old man said, "We are the Ottomans. Our empire has just recently joined this war." Hans remembered hearing about them at the Aisne so long ago. These men were much different than the Germans. Instead of a pickelhaube, they wore what appeared to be a cloth hat. Instead of blond hair, they had black hair. Their uniforms were the color of sand, while the German uniform was gray.

The man noticed this too, and said, "You will be an easy target for the British. Come. Let's get you a new uniform." The man led him into the dugout. Inside were a few uniforms. Hans put one of them on, along with the hat they called a *Kabalak.* Then, the rest of the crew walked in. They all looked at each other and smiled. They were all wounded but alive. They were led to another dugout, with beds for them to sleep. Hans lay in one of the beds, and was instantly asleep.

Hans was by Heinrich's cross in the field. A ghostly figure stood behind it. It was Heinrich.

"You are a failure. I am dead because of you," Heinrich said.

"No. There was nothing I could do. You're lying," Hans said with great sadness.

Heinrich's eyes turned blood red, and he said, "Mark my words Hans, because of this, you and your crew will see Hell." He opened his hand, and a picture materialized. There was fire and mud and blood. Corpses were everywhere. There was screaming and moaning. Heinrich closed his hand. Then, he turned pale. His fingers grew claws. He opened his mouth, revealing twisted fangs and a forked tongue. His hair fell out, and two horns sprouted out of his head.

"I look forward to seeing you in Hell," the Devil boomed, and then lunged, killing Hans. Hans woke up, his heart racing.

That was a very strange dream, Hans thought, *I guess I do feel guilty about Heinrich's death, but I had nothing to do with it.* Hans pondered the dream for a long while before realizing it was morning. He got out of bed and left the dugout, looking around for the old man.

Once he found him, Hans asked, "Where can I find a rifle?" The man nodded and led him to a dugout, where he was given a Turkish Mauser. For some reason, there was a feeling of tenseness in the air. Then, he saw a glint on the horizon. Suddenly, an Ottoman fell, a bullet through his head.

The old man turned to Hans and said, "It is time. You must prepare for battle. They are coming."

Chapter 14
The Sands of Death

The attack had begun. Hans saw a group of horses charging at the trenches. The soldiers on them were yelling as they held cavalry swords high. Hans shot at one of the men, and he fell off his horse. There were few Ottoman machine guns, but there were enough to hold off the first wave. But there was a second wave. They heard loud booms as the artillery fired. They all quickly retreated to the dugouts before the shells hit. Many of the weaker dugouts collapsed, and most of their machine guns were obliterated. Hans climbed out of the dugout as soon as the barrage was finished. He was alarmed to find that British soldiers were halfway to the trenches. This time, the Ottomans struggled to hold the line. A few of the British made it to the trenches. A soldier was about to stab Hans with his bayonet, but Hans was quicker. He slammed the man on the head with the stock of his rifle. The man fell backward, unconscious. Hans quickly killed him with a bullet to his brain at point-blank range. Over and over, the British soldiers charged, and every time, the Ottomans grew weaker and weaker. The sand in the trenches was no longer orange; it was red with blood. The British knew they were winning, and that confidence enforced their attack. When Hans saw the sixth wave, he was sure it would be the last, one way or the other. As they neared the trenches, Hans threw his bolt-action weapon aside, and picked up a British semi-automatic gun. The corpses of the first wave's horses provided cover for the British. Those poor horses were reduced to pieces of flesh, bone, and blood. Hans shot man after man, but there were too many of them. He picked up another semi-automatic rifle, and wielded the two guns. The Ottomans saw what Hans was doing, and copied him. The British were infiltrating the trenches. Hans retreated into a dugout with some other Ottomans, providing them with cover. A grenade rolled into the dugout. An Ottoman was about to throw the grenade back, but it exploded, blowing off his arm. They were cornered in the dugout. They could not run. Many of the Ottomans were killed, but not in vain. The British had lost many men. There wouldn't be another wave. They fought, and they fought, and then, the guns fell silent. They had done it. The British were dead. Only four soldiers remained in the dugout. Hans turned to the three other Ottomans and nodded before they climbed out of the dugout. So many Ottomans lay dead. He suddenly heard yelling by a collapsed dugout. Hans picked up a shovel from a corpse and dug into the sand. He found his crew and a few Ottomans. They climbed out of the dugout.

They didn't even talk to each other. They all knew what to do. Hans walked along the trench, looking for any collapsed dugouts. Then he saw something that stopped him in his tracks. He saw the old man lying on the ground. He was mutilated. His face had been horribly disfigured. His intestines spilled out over his uniform. There was so much blood. He was almost unrecognizable. It sickened Hans to see the kind old man murdered so gruesomely. Hans tried not to vomit as he walked through the carnage. It was the most death he had ever seen. He became even more convinced that the British were nothing more than savages. He noticed that all the Ottomans were mutilated, disfigured, or both. However, the British either had a single bullet in their head or a few holes in their gut. Hans was by no means racist, but after seeing this, he was sure that their people were the host of the Devil. The things they had done were unforgivable. Hans prayed to God that all these British scum would go to Hell. War is terrible, but to Hans, it seemed completely unnecessary to do this to people. He finally found a collapsed dugout. As he dug, he found a couple of Ottomans who had suffocated. By the time midday rolled around, Hans had saved 19 Ottomans. He looked around; full of pride for having saved these men. He noticed a British soldier lying against the trench. His eyes were glassy, and he was near the end of his life, but he was breathing. Hans wanted so badly to get revenge, but he decided against it. If he mutilated this man, he was no better than the British that had done the same to the Ottomans. He decided to do what was right. This man would die, either way, so Hans decided to relieve him of his pain. He put a bullet in his head. After looking at the dead man for some time, Hans stood up. They had won the battle, but at what cost? In some areas, he couldn't even see the bottom of the trench; it was covered by bodies. The desert heat made the smell of rotting corpses unbearable. Hans started digging a mass grave. After a bit, the Ottomans joined in. Though they didn't speak German, and Hans didn't speak Turkish, they still knew why they were digging. After an hour, it was ready. Hans walked out of the dugout, grabbed a corpse, and carried it to the grave. They worked all day and into the night until it was finished. Hans was sweating badly and began to feel dizzy. He knew why. Dehydration. He figured it would find him one way or another in the desert. He needed water but, it was too late. Hans collapsed. He used what little energy he had to yell for one of the crew members before blacking out.

"Hans! Hans!" Someone yelled. Hans couldn't make out who it was, but he slowly opened his eyes. He was lying on his back, and somebody was pouring water from a canteen into his mouth. The warm water rolled down his esophagus. It revived him. He was still dizzy, but he managed to stand. It was only then that he realized who had saved his life. Fritz. Hans would have cried, but he had no tears. He embraced Fritz.

"You saved my life," Hans said.

"You would have done the same for me, friend," said Fritz. One of the reasons Hans was so grateful was that Fritz could have left him to die. Instead, Fritz gave Hans the most precious thing in the desert, water. Hans looked at Fritz one last time and saluted.

Fritz gave him a wide grin and returned the salute. Hans remembered what kind of person he was before the war. He was wise, intelligent, and kind to others. But he was also slightly naive, even after seeing the horrors of the world. He had thought he'd seen the worst of humanity. Now, looking back on it, he realized just how wrong he was. This war would scar him for life. He had seen things that nobody should ever have to see. He sometimes lost faith in God because he wondered how any god could let these terrible things happen. But he would always remember that if there is a God, there is the Devil. The evil he had seen often made him think of the Devil. Everyone has evil inside of them, and this war proved it. They killed their own species without a second thought. But Hans had done a good thing here. He had buried the dead. Whether they were British or Ottoman, they all deserved to be buried. Before the grave was covered, Hans had counted 568 corpses.

As night set in, the desert grew cold. The bodies had all been buried, finally giving Hans time to rest. He and the rest of his crew walked into a dugout that held weapons. They sat on the floor and told each other stories about the battle and what happened after it. They talked until they could hardly keep their eyes open. They decided to sleep, knowing they had a long day ahead of them. They always did.

It was still dark, but Wilhelm woke Hans up. Wilhelm gestured for him to be quiet, and he pointed outside. Hans listened carefully, footsteps. He quickly looked outside the dugout. British soldiers. They were walking through the trench. Hans reached for his gun, but Wilhelm shook his head. Wilhelm took the rifle and silently took the bayonet off. He gave it to Hans, and then took the bayonet off of another rifle. Wilhelm pointed to the front corners of the dugout. The entrance was between them. Now Hans understood. He slowly crept to the left corner. Wilhelm went to the right corner. The footsteps drew closer. The soldiers silently entered the dugout. There were two of them. They each had knives. They crept towards the sleeping crew. Hans and Wilhelm struck. Hans leaped forward, and thrust his bayonet into one of the soldiers. The man arched his back, let out a yell, and crumpled to the ground. Wilhelm had dealt with the other man. Hans made sure to finish the job, and he stabbed the man in the back of the head. By now, the rest of the crew was awake. Fritz stared at Hans with wide eyes.

"You saved me," Fritz muttered.

"No. No, I didn't," Hans said, "Don't thank me. Wilhelm here is the one that saved us all." The crew thanked

Wilhelm. Hans smiled, realizing that Wilhelm may have saved the entire group of Ottomans. Then, he came to a grave realization. They wouldn't have been the first dugout the Brits would have visited. Hans ran out of their dugout and into the nearest one to them.

"Son of a bitch," Hans said as he saw the inside of the dugout. The Ottomans lay on their backs; their throats cut wide open and gushing blood. They had saved themselves, but not the others. Hans ran down the entire trench. Dead. All of them. Thankfully, the crew had been in the middle of the trench, meaning that the Ottomans on the other half were still alive. Hans let out a sigh of relief and distress. He walked back to the dugout.

"Wilhelm," Hans said, "You saved more than just us." Wilhelm gave Hans a confused look.

"What do you mean?" He asked

"Everyone on the right part of the trench is dead," Hans informed, "but everyone on the left side is alive. You saved half of our army."

Wilhelm's eyes widened, and he cleared his throat before replying "We should probably get back to sleep. I'll take guard duty."

Chapter 15
Despair and Beauty

Morning dawned. Hans slowly stood up and stretched. He was incredibly sore from sleeping on the ground. Wilhelm and Frank were still sleeping, for they had guarded the crew during the night. Hans stepped out of the dugout and was assaulted by the light and heat of the desert sun, which he had come to hate. Hans saw a general talking to some of the Ottomans.

"That's General Ahmed Djemal Pasha. I saw pictures of him when they joined the war," Fritz said from behind. Hans looked back at Fritz and smiled, then turned back toward General Pasha. The soldiers saluted him and left for a dugout. Hans decided to see what they were doing. Fritz followed him. What they saw greatly surprised them. Inside the dugout, there was an underground passage leading toward the British lines. When Hans approached them, he wrote a question mark in the sand. The men nodded, and they drew something. It was their lines and the British lines. There was a passage leading to the British trench. Under the British trench, a stick figure was placing something. Then they destroyed the drawing and made the gesture for an explosion. Hans understood. The Ottomans started walking toward the end of the passage. Hans and Fritz grabbed shovels and followed them. They walked for a while before they came to the end. The Ottomans started to dig, so Hans and Fritz helped them. They dug all day. Then, they found the trench. A bit of the ground caved in, revealing it. The Ottomans ran down the passage, presumably to get the explosives. Hans and Fritz ducked below the hole in the passage. They heard someone walking toward them. A man stuck his head through the hole. Hans stabbed the man in his throat, severing his jugular. Fritz dragged the man into the passage and snapped his neck. They waited for about a minute, and then heard the Ottomans. They had a wheelbarrow full of barrels of gunpowder. When they reached the end of the passage, they turned around and ran toward the Ottoman lines. Hans and Fritz quickly followed them. Hans saw one of the men produce a clay incendiary grenade. He threw it down the passage. Crack. BOOOOOOOM.

The entire camp exploded. The Ottomans cheered. Everyone was thrilled. This would give the Ottomans plenty of time to prepare for another attack. The British camp was now just a heap of fire and metal. The soldiers laughed and clapped. They celebrated the rest of the day. That night, Herman, Frank, and Hans watched over the crew. For the next few weeks, they worked with the Ottomans to reinforce their positions with what they had. December rolled in, and Hans felt homesick when he remembered how beautiful Berlin looked in the winter. He missed having snowball fights with Carl and building snowmen with his family. He had so many good memories. He missed spending time with Alice. Christmas was coming, and he was sad he would be spending it in the trenches. Then, in mid-December, the British returned. Hans was playing cards with the crew when he heard the artillery. There were no Ottoman casualties; they had built new and better dugouts. Then came the troops. The cavalry led the charge once again. Hans made sure to target the horses. He was sad to do it, but it was necessary. However, the British had a few tricks up their sleeves as well. A few of the horses made it to the trenches. It was then that Hans realized nobody was riding the horses. They were dummies. It happened instantly. BOOOM. The horses exploded, and so did the dummies. All along the trenches, Ottomans were blown apart. Next, the British pounded the camp with artillery. The Ottomans couldn't hold off the British and survive the artillery. They only had one option— retreat.

General Pasha yelled, "Retreat! Retreat!" Hans understood what he said because, over the past few weeks, the Ottoman soldiers taught him words used on the battlefield. The army began to retreat. They had to flee to the rocky hills behind the Ottoman camp. Hans heard a soldier yell into a radio, "Requesting backup! Requesting backu..." The man was shot in the head before he could finish the call for help. The army ran through the camp, heading for the hills. Hans sprinted toward the hills too. The only good thing was that the British didn't have any heavy machine guns. Some of the wounded struggled to continue and were killed. Hans was about halfway up the hill when he was shot in his hand. He lost his grip and tumbled down the rocky formation. Taking out his PO8, which had been given to him by the Ottomans, he killed a few of the Brits before starting the climb back up. Bullets whizzed past him as he climbed. Hans saw the body of an Ottoman a few feet up. His unblinking eyes stared down at him. He was almost there. Hans climbed as fast as he could. Finally, he reached the top before almost half of the army. He encouraged the men to keep climbing and helped them. Soon the entirety of the army had made it to the top of the hills. They ran down the other side of the hills as fast as they could. The wounded were left behind. Waiting for them would slow down the army. Hans ran down the hill and saw what was ahead of them. Desert. The regiment was doomed. They would never survive the heat and the might of the strongest country in the world with no supplies. But, then Hans saw it. Reinforcements.

German armored cars drove through the sand at full speed. He just had to survive a bit longer. As the British crested the hills, the armored cars fired at them. However, they were too far away, and only a few of the bullets hit. After holding off the Brits for a few more minutes, the vehicles arrived. There were 20 of them. It was then that

Hans realized the problem. There were about 250 Ottomans. Hans quickly climbed into one of the vehicles before there was no room. In just a few minutes, all the vehicles were packed. There was no more room, and the 47 Ottomans left outside banged on the vehicles, crying and yelling. Hans felt so sorry for them, but there was nothing they could do. The British just kept coming. As the vehicles pulled away, the men who'd made it in screamed at the drivers with tears rolling down their faces. Hans couldn't bring himself to look back at the stranded men. Instead, he asked Wilhelm, who was right next to him, where they were headed.

"Probably Constantinople," Wilhelm answered. It was the capital of the Ottoman Empire. After hearing this, Hans was quiet. They sat in the vehicle for what felt like years. When they arrived in Constantinople, there was a lot of chaos as men were rushed to a hospital. Hans and the crew had no idea where to go, and nobody spoke their language. Luckily, they found the beach. Hans and the crew walked to a dock and saw a fishing boat. A young man was smoking by the dock. Hans knew he was Ottoman, so he didn't bother trying to talk to him. Instead, he pointed toward the fishing boat, then at the man. The man nodded, and he pointed at Hans with a quizzical look. Wilhelm took out a map and gave it to Hans. Hans pointed to Germany. He then dragged his finger to France. The man nodded, and then tapped his hand, as if expecting payment. The crew looked at each other, trying to think of a way to pay this man. Finally, Herman sighed and took something out of his pocket. It was a golden pocket watch. Herman opened it up. The clock inside of it worked perfectly. There was also a picture inside. It was of Herman standing by a beautiful young woman. He gave the watch to the man. The man stared at it with a wide grin on his face. Then it faded. He looked at Herman, and then at the watch. He took out the picture and gave it to Herman. They both looked at each other and smiled. The man stepped aside and gestured to the boat. The crew hopped aboard. After a few minutes, the boat was on its way. The crew went below decks to the bunks. "Herman, how did you get that watch, and who was the woman in the picture?" Hans asked.

Herman hesitated for a moment, before saying, "The woman's name is Eva. We first met in a diner about three years ago. We got married in 1913. She knew I wasn't very wealthy, so she decided to give me a gift. It was that watch. You see, her family was very wealthy. As for the picture, it was taken a few weeks before the war. I don't know what I'm going to say when I go home to her, and she sees I don't have the watch. But, I knew we needed to get back home."

Everyone sat in silence for a bit, before Wilhelm said, "Thank you. You gave away your most prized possession so we could go home." After that statement, the whole crew thanked Herman. They all started to tell each other about their lives. The most interesting story was Wilhelm's. As the oldest of the crew, he had the most to say. Night fell, and they looked out the windows. They saw the exotic island of Crete. It had beautiful white beaches, and even at night, Hans could tell that the water was a dazzling turquoise. He saw the small towns lining the coast and palm trees, whose leaves waved at the fishing boat. The entire crew fantasized about living there. They could jump off the boat and swim there, and lay on the beach together in peace forever. But they had a duty. Germany needed them. They had to fight until their last breath, as Heinrich did. They couldn't run away from this war. No, this war was different. It was a world war. .

"I think I'm going to get some rest," Hans said, and went to sleep.

Hans was running through a hallway. He was covered in blood, and he felt very weak, but he continued. He ran into a concrete room where people were standing over a map. One of them seemed vaguely familiar. Hans took out a pistol and shot at the man. The bullet missed. Then, someone ran into the room from behind him and hit him with the barrel of his rifle. Hans fell over and dropped his pistol. The man flipped him over. It was Fritz. He put the gun to Hans's head.

As soon as Hans woke, he forgot the dream. It was morning, and he smelled something delicious, so he decided to investigate. In the kitchen, Hans found the captain cooking some fish for the crew. Hans then went to the deck of the boat. It was a sunny day with clear skies. In the distance, he saw a few islands.

"Beautiful day, isn't it?" Wilhelm said from behind.

"Yes, it is, friend," Hans said.

"Heinrich and I were friends as kids, you know," said Wilhelm.

"I didn't know that," Hans said.

"Yes. As kids, we would always play on the streets together. He went to my house sometimes. His mother was an alcoholic, and she sometimes beat him. There were times where he stayed at our home for days at a time. He would sometimes sit on our doorstep after being beaten. I would come out and comfort him, and we would talk for hours. Once, he ran over to my house with his arm dripping blood. We had to take him to the hospital. Later, he told me that his mother had thrown a bottle at him. As we got older, he began to stand up to his mother. She continued to abuse him, but he didn't run. He would plead to his mother to get help. She never listened. Eventually, she committed suicide. His father died from grief a week later. His father had done little to help young Heinrich during his life, for he had to work to keep food on the table. After that, we invited him to live with us. He refused. He didn't want to siphon our family's money. He went to live on the streets. He would visit us every so often whenever he had spare time. He was a good friend. I miss him."

“I miss him too, Wilhelm,” Hans said sympathetically. They leaned against the guard rail of the ship, and they stared out at the Mediterranean.

“It sure is beautiful,” Wilhelm said.

“Yea, it is. Really takes your mind off of the trenches,” Hans observed.

“It does. I hate those trenches. The things I’ve seen in there....I’ll never forget,” Wilhelm mumbled. The memories suddenly attacked Hans. He saw the blood and the bodies. Hans grew pale, and almost vomited. He was shaking. Then, he put his head in his hands and sobbed.

“So...young...bodies...death...blood,” Hans rambled. Wilhelm put his hand on Hans’s shoulder.

“It’s okay; you’re going to be okay. Don’t let it get to your head. It’s okay. I’m here for you,” Wilhelm said empathetically. He was no stranger to this. Then, the captain rang a bell. Immediately, the two friends went below decks and into the kitchen. The crew was seated at the table. They sat in silence as they ate their fish, for they all knew something was wrong. When they had all finished eating, Hans walked into the bunks. He didn’t want to live anymore. Despair consumed him. His whole life, he had suffered. He took out his pistol and put it to his head. His finger began to squeeze the trigger.

“No!” Wilhelm screamed as he tackled Hans. BAM. The bullet shattered a window. Wilhelm ripped the gun out of Hans’s hand. “How could you?” Wilhelm yelled. Hans sobbed. He couldn’t believe that he had almost killed himself. He looked at Wilhelm with tears in his eyes. Wilhelm looked at Hans, and his anger turned to sympathy.

"Hans, you have to put this behind you. We're here for you. Me and Fritz and Frank and Herman all care about you. We're like brothers. Please don't end your life. When the war is over, we'll be here for you. Promise me you won't do this again, Hans. Promise me. I beg you."

Hans was silent for a moment, before saying, "I...I... promise."

Wilhelm sat down next to Hans.

"You know, when I was in Samoa, I had a friend named Rodrigo. One day we were marching through the jungles when he stepped on a landmine. I couldn't save him. That day I wished I could have died with him. But now, many years later, I have learned something. That could have been me who died. I wasted so many years wanting to be dead with him when I didn't realize how precious life is. Don't make the mistake I did, Hans. Your life is too precious." Hans thought about his words. He had been so consumed by grief; he hadn't realized that through all his pain and suffering and despair, he was still alive. He had survived the horrors of war. He had survived the slaughter and the murder and the gore. Then, Hans grinned and started to laugh. He ran up to the deck, over to the guard rail, and threw out his arms. As the wind whipped through his hair, he realized that he was grateful for life. He looked into the sky, and he could practically see Heinrich and Carl and Alice and his father smiling down at him. He had found happiness. He realized Wilhelm was staring at him and laughing.

"You did it, Hans. You have learned to love life. You have found happiness," Wilhelm said, and embraced Hans. After a few minutes, the rest of the crew joined them, and they sang songs in joy. As they did so, they watched the boat head for a dock in Spain. Soon the boat docked, and the captain left. They knew he needed to get fuel. They noticed that Spain was only slightly different from Crete. There were many other types of trees, and the buildings were less crude. The water was also less clear, but still beautiful. The man came back with eight barrels of fuel. He also bought Blackjack for the crew. As the boat turned toward the Strait of Gibraltar, the crew went below decks to set up Blackjack on the kitchen table. They played for hours, and Herman won every time.

"How are you so good at this?" Fritz asked in frustration.

"My father was a master of this game. One day I asked him that very same question. He then spent the rest of the day teaching me all the tricks," Herman answered.

Hans immediately asked, "Can you teach us some of these so-called 'tricks'?"

"If I did, the game would be no fun," Herman replied.

"Actually, it's no fun if you keep beating us. If you told us all your tricks, we would all have an equal chance of winning. You just don't want to lose, do you?" Wilhelm asked.

Herman was unable to find words. Wilhelm smiled.

“No…No I’m...I’m not afraid to…to lose. I’ll...I’ll teach you the tricks,” Herman stuttered, embarrassed. They spent the next half hour learning his tricks. They were ready. They would play one final game. They bickered amongst themselves what the reward would be for the winner. They decided that the winner would get half of everyone’s dinner. The game had begun. Everyone was tense and concentrating. All Hans could hear was the tik tok, tik tok from the clock on the wall. When he had to speak, he couldn’t even hear himself; the words simply floated out of his mouth. Herman showed everyone his cards. He had a score of 19. Hans let out a big sigh as he only had 17. Wilhelm had 18. Frank had 15. Then, Fritz smiled. He showed Herman his cards. 20. He had won. Herman stared at Fritz, his mouth wide open.

“You’re a good player, Herman, but it turns out that you’re a better teacher,” Fritz said. The whole crew looked at Herman and started to laugh. Herman was fuming, but eventually, he too began to laugh.

“I taught you how to play better than I can,” Herman said, laughing hysterically. When it was time to eat, the captain once again made them fish. Everyone but Fritz solemnly cut their fillet in half. He grinned as they all gave him his winnings and when he saw how much he would get to eat. As they began to eat, Fritz told them about his life as a fisherman before the war. It had been his pride and joy. Though he didn’t get much income from it, he felt it was enough. He told them how his favorite river to fish at was the Würm River. He always caught many fish there. However, about two weeks before the war, he had gotten a new job as a mechanic, though he wasn't qualified. There he learned to drive machines. When they were finished eating, they went up to the main deck and stood by the guard rail. They watched the sun set over the sea. The sky was beautiful, and looked painted with so many different colors. They watched the sky until the sun went completely below the horizon. Hans went to the sleeping quarters early. He lay in bed, staring at the ceiling, thinking about his life. So much had happened to him in his 24-years, it was amazing. He was only one man, and yet he had killed and saved so many. He had changed the tide of battles, escaped death itself, and been across multiple fronts of the war. When he died, he would be remembered. He was sure of it. When the war was over, people would never forget it. They would not forget.

He would never realize how wrong he was.

Chapter 16
The Return to France

Hans woke up with a start. He didn't remember when he had fallen asleep. He realized that the boat was rocking much more than usual and quickly ran to the main deck. There he saw a red sky. Dark clouds were advancing on the boat. The waves had gotten much bigger, and they slammed into the boat. They were in a storm. Hail rained down on the boat, damaging it.

"Hans get below decks," Wilhelm yelled. Hans could barely hear him over the howling wind. A chunk of ice hit Hans in his shoulder, knocking him to the ground. The deck became slick as the cold water splashed onto it. Hans managed to glance at the captain. He was struggling to steer as the hail pelted him. He crawled towards the stairs. Suddenly, the boat hit a rock, and Hans was thrown forward and down the stairs. He slowly stood up.

"Hans," Wilhelm yelled at him, "We're taking on water. We need to bail." Hans nodded, and Wilhelm led him to the sleeping quarters. The floorboards had splintered, leaving a gaping hole. Water was pouring into the boat at an alarming rate. Hans looked around and saw that there were no buckets to be found. There was only one option. Hans took his hands, cupped them, and scooped some of the water up. He quickly ran to the main deck and threw the water off the ship. It would be impossible to keep the boat floating. When he ran back downstairs, there was twice as much water as there had been before. Then, he got an idea.

"Close the door!" Hans yelled at the crew, "We can isolate the water if we close the door." The crew agreed. They quickly ran out of the sleeping quarters and slammed the door shut. The water simply went under the door. Hans ran to the kitchen and grabbed all of the towels he could find. He ran back to the door and stuffed them under the crack. It held the water back. It was temporary, but it would work for now. Hans ran back up to the deck. He couldn't see the end of the clouds. Suddenly, a huge wave slammed into the side of the boat, sending a wave of freezing water onto the deck. Hans was swept off his feet, and thrown over the side of the boat. He was barely hanging on to the guard rail but began to lose his grip. He saw a pile of rope hanging by the guard rail, and, using the last of his energy, he grabbed it and tied it around himself. He tied the other end to the railing and let go. As he fell, he prayed that the rope would hold. He was pulled under the freezing water and it dragged him down deeper. The rope tightened and squeezed all the air out of him, but he smiled in relief because it held. However, he was being pulled around in the water, hanging only by a rope, with no oxygen. Hans knew what he had to do. He opened his eyes and looked toward the boat. He grabbed the length of rope above him and started to pull himself up. He was sure that three things could kill him right then: the lack of oxygen, the cold, or the pain. The rope cut into his hands, and he saw blood seeping into the water. But he had to climb. He was exhausted, but he had to do it, or he would die. His lungs pleaded for air to no avail. Hans was so drained, but he knew if he closed his eyes, he would never wake up. He was only halfway there. The first layer of skin on his hands was gone. Hans's vision turned fuzzy. His lungs kept trying to get him to open his mouth and take a breath of air, but he resisted. There was no air. He looked up at the ship. It was sinking. He was so close, but he was so cold and so tired. Using his last bit of energy, he thrust his hand out of the water, but he was too tired, and his muscles gave out. He was slipping back down. Suddenly, someone grabbed his hand. Wilhelm pulled Hans's limp body up onto the deck. Hans could only hear a bit of what the crew was saying. "Hans, Are you okay?"

"What's wrong with him?"

"Lack of oxygen," Wilhelm answered.

"Is he alive?" someone asked, but then Hans lost consciousness.

Moments later, Hans opened his eyes and, when he realized that he was on the deck, started taking in huge breaths of air. He tried to stand. He looked at his hands. They were severely cut, and blood dripped onto the deck. He was freezing but realized he wasn't shivering. He untied the rope from his waist.

"Hans, you're going into shock, and you have moderate hypothermia. You need heat fast, or you may not make it back to the trenches alive," Wilhelm ordered. The problem was that they were wearing clothes meant for the Ottoman Empire. They were very light and provided no extra warmth. The hail turned into freezing rain. Suddenly, Wilhelm had an idea. He ran below decks and grabbed the captain's gun, and he ran back up to Hans. Then, Wilhelm fired a shot. As he pulled the bolt, a shell casing shot out onto the deck. "Hans pick it up," Wilhelm instructed. "But it's hot," Hans said in confusion, "It'll burn me."

"Hans, you're confused. You don't know what's going on. Pick up the shell. It'll provide you heat," Wilhelm yelled. Hans still didn't understand, but he picked up the shell casing. Hans smiled as the heat warmed his battered and numb hands. The boat leaned sideways. They had a few minutes at best. The engine became waterlogged, preventing the ship from getting any closer to the shore. They stood on deck until the boat neared sinking, firing shells to keep Hans warm. It wasn't nearly enough, but it saved his life. The captain ran to them, and pointed to Belgium. They had to jump off the boat. They noticed that the captain wasn't shivering either and looked at him in concern, but he ignored them. They were about 300 feet from the shore. They gave each other one last look and then jumped into the water. Immediately upon entering the cold water, Hans's muscles began to seize up. However, he knew he had to swim for shore, so he did. Everyone reached the shore, except for the captain. When the crew pulled him out of the water, his eyes were glassy, and he didn't have a pulse. They left his body on the beach. After being in the freezing water once again, Hans was even colder than before. They walked through the snow for a while before finding a cave. They all huddled inside of it to get some warmth. They found some twigs, and Fritz used a couple of the larger ones, to make a bow drill. He started a small fire. Hans took off his wet shirt and hat and used them as fuel for the fire. The rest of the crew did the same. Soon, however, the fire ran out of fuel, and it died. They only had two options. Stay in the cave and wait for help, or look for civilization and risk death from hypothermia. They all knew what they had to do. They walked out of the cave and were on their way. After a few minutes, they saw them—the trenches. As soon as they saw the spike of a pickelhaube, they ran to them as fast as they could. When they jumped into them, they met a German wearing a winter coat.

"What the hell are you people doing out here in the cold? Come on, we'll get you bunch some winter clothes," the man said, and he led them into a small dugout. They were given guns and winter clothes. When Hans climbed out of the dugout, he saw a French soldier climbing out of the trench, and he took aim. Suddenly, the man tackled him.

"Are you crazy?" the man yelled at him, "Our armies have declared a truce."

Chapter 17
Weihnachten

"A truce?" Hans asked in confusion, "But this is war."

"No," the man said angrily. "The war is going on, but we've decided on a ceasefire." Hans nodded and stood up. He set his gun along the side of the trench. He walked over to some soldiers and helped them set tannenbaums along the front of the trench. Suddenly, he heard something coming from the British trenches.

"Silent night, holy night,
All is calm, all is bright
Round yon virgin mother and child.
Holy Infant, so tender and mild,
Sleep in heavenly peace.
Sleep in heavenly peace." Then something echoed it.

"Stille Nacht, Heil'ge Nacht,
Alles schlaft, Einsam wacht
Nur das traute heilige Paar.
Holder Knab' im lockigen Haar;
Schlafe in himmlischer Ruh,
Schlafe in himmlischer Ruh." This repeated.

The armies were trying to sing over one another. Hans joined in as the Germans tried to drown out the Brits. Eventually, they sang in harmony. They also sang *O Christmas Tree*. Then, the most amazing thing happened. A German jumped out of the trench. He walked across no man's land. Some of the British reached for their guns, but after they saw the man was unarmed, they changed their minds. When the man reached their lines, he said something that warmed the hearts of every soldier.

The man said in British, "Merry Christmas." There was silence. Then, Hans saw the men smile. The man returned to his trench, but this had set off a chain of events Hans decided to do something. He opened the gift he had received from the Kaiser. Inside was a bar of chocolate. Hans grabbed it and left the trench. A British soldier saw what he was doing, and he did the same. They met in the middle of no man's land. Hans looked at the man and gave him the chocolate. The man gave him a pack of cigarettes. Hans smiled at him and realized something. These were people. Hans had spent so much time killing them that he had forgotten something very important. No matter how savage they were, they were human beings. Hans looked into the man's eyes, and he saw humanity. He saw a loving father with a wife and children. He saw a man with feelings and opinions. That day, all the clouds of sadness and anger cleared away, and life shined through. Now, Hans wanted this war to end. Didn't the commanders realize how happy they were without war? This war had torn families apart, stripped men of their dignity, and taken the lives of so many of a generation. They had fought for half a year. This war needed to be over. Sadly, the leaders of their countries didn't agree. Hans shook the man's hand and turned around. He saw all the bodies on the battlefield. It was time to bury these poor souls. Hans climbed back into the trench and grabbed a shovel. He went back to the corpses. He planted the shovel into the ground, and he beckoned to his crew. They came to Hans with shovels. "We're going to bury the dead," Hans informed them, "and they get their own graves. They deserve better than a common grave." Hans looked down at the corpse of a faceless man and then started to dig a grave. Soon both armies joined in, and by night, the dead all had their separate graves. When Hans went back to the German trenches, he opened the pack of cigarettes that the British soldier had given him. He took out a lighter that he had been provided with his new uniform, and he lit one of them. Hans was not a smoker, for he had heard of some of its harmful effects, but he decided that just a few during Christmas wouldn't hurt him. As the crew met up in a dugout, Hans saw what they had all gotten. Fritz and Wilhelm had also gotten a pack of cigarettes, while Frank and Herman had gotten plum pudding. All through the night, they celebrated and sang carols with the British, for they were all too giddy to sleep.

In the morning, Hans was walking through the trench, when a man ran up to him.

"Are you Hans Fitzgerald?" the man asked.

"Yes, sir. What do you need?" Hans responded.

"You have a letter from someone named Frieda Sonnen," the man answered.

"Frieda Sonnen? I've never heard of her," Hans said in confusion.

"Well, just take the letter," the man said, "It's for you." Hans sighed, and he took the letter. He walked into a dugout, sat down, and opened the letter with a knife.

Dear Hans

My name is Frieda Sonnen, which I'm sure you found out from the person who has given this to you. Anyway, I am Carl's mother. He often told me about you when he was alive. You seemed like a very nice man. I felt very worried when I heard about you and your crew. I just wanted to wish you luck, and I pray you make it out of the war alive. There is also a picture for you. Carl would draw it in his spare time. I wish you luck, Hans. Carl would be proud of you.

Hans stared at the letter, his eyes wide and his mouth open. Then he took the picture out. When he saw it, he began to cry. It was a drawing of him. The only thing that was unfinished was his arm. It was so full of detail; Hans was heartbroken. They had been like brothers. A single tear splattered onto the drawing. Hans looked at it, and he saw Carl in the tear.

Carl looked at Hans and said, “Hans, let it go. I will always be here for you.” Hans sighed and knew it was the truth. He stood up and walked outside. He saw two commanders standing in no man’s land. They raised their pistols into the air and fired a single shot.

“And so the war begins,” Fritz said from behind Hans. Hans looked back at Fritz and gave him a sad smile. The commanders jumped back into their respective trenches. The German commander yelled at the soldiers, “This truce is over. You will pick up your guns and fight.” Hans wanted to resist, but he would face prosecution if he did. He walked to the side of the trench and picked up his gun. He aimed at a British soldier.

BAM.

Author's Note

First of all, I would like to thank all the people who read this book before it was published. Their feedback helped me finish this book. The strange thing is that I actually got the inspiration to write this book after playing a video game about WW1 a few years back. It taught me most of the lessons I depicted in this book. I wrote this book for two reasons. The first was a reminder. Over the years, we have forgotten the Great War. The only war Americans care about nowadays is WW2. The only reason people know WW1 even exists is because if there was a WW2, there must have been a WW1. It greatly saddens me to tell you this, but it's true. This book shows the suffering we forgot. When I was younger, I went to a history museum. One of the floors was called "America's Greatest Generation." It was about WW2. Merely by naming it that, that museum disrespected millions of dead soldiers. That entire museum didn't have *one* exhibit about WW1! I left that museum angry but inspired. That visit was like fuel to my fiery passion for keeping this war alive. The next reason I wrote this book was perspective. We as Americans tend to consider our side 'the good side.' Many think that everything we do is right. Most American authors like to write about America or her Allies. This is incredibly biased. That's why I decided to write about the Germans. When Americans think about Germany, they often think only of Adolf Hitler. Even some of my best friends think that because that one man was 'bad', all Germans are bad. This is completely untrue. Most Americans are very uncomfortable with standing up for Germany. I would like you to keep in mind that Hitler only rose to power because of the Allies, or the Triple Entente as it was called. This is because of one thing: the Treaty of Versailles. That treaty doomed what could have been European peace. It blamed the entire war on Germany. This was and is completely unacceptable. This war was started by the Allies, specifically Serbia. The Treaty of Versailles put Germany in massive, and I mean *massive,* debt. With Germany in economic ruin, anybody could have risen to power. Hitler did because of his speaking abilities. Also, to Germany at the time, the Nazis were a clean slate for the country. Hitler knew this, and when he talked about invading other countries, the Germans had no problem with it. After all, it was the only way to get out of debt and save this dying country. Kids in Germany would play with hundreds of wads of money because of how little value it had. And so, WW2 began. This book strove to teach perspective. There is no 'good' or 'bad' side. It just depends on how one sees something. I tried to teach this by showing the perspective of Germany. Please remember that whatever country we belong to, we are all human. We absolutely should not disrespect the dead from other countries, even if we don't fight with them.

There are some things in my book that are historically inaccurate. I'll explain these inaccuracies, chapter by chapter.

Chapter one gave a great start to the book, and it didn't have many, if any, inaccuracies.

Chapter two is where there are some historical mistakes. First of all, Hans's odds of survival in this chapter would have been extremely low, and I'm not sure if he would have won the Iron Cross. Now, as my excuse for many of these inaccuracies and the answer as to how he met Hitler, the chances are incredibly low but possible. I also did this to show that Adolf Hitler fought in the Great War or WW1. Now for the elephant, or should I say, the tank in the room. I know perfectly well that the A7V tank was not made until 1918, and it didn't have Big Bertha on it (the large gun on the top), but I simply did these two things to provide the book with excitement. And the coordinates on the note do not provide an exact location at the Marne. In chapter three, Hans fires the huge gun for the first time. My excuse for how this massive piece of artillery is loaded by one man is just the evil plot convenience. I don't know if it's mathematically possible to even do this.

As chapter four takes the novice crew to Paris, I'm sure there is not an underground cave connecting the Marne to Paris. Now, the reason why Hans passes out is partially due to his mild concussion. However, this cave is also filled with contaminated air with hallucinogenic properties caused by the crystals. This is why only Hans passes out. Also, as far as I know, there isn't a large oil rig under the Eiffel Tower, but I wouldn't put it past any government to cover it up.

In chapter five, we get our first look at the HMS Snow. This dreadnought is completely fictional, but the paint on it symbolizes the cholera outbreak of 1854. Also, a dreadnought likely wouldn't be able to navigate the Seine. The main other inaccuracy is the anti-tank gun, which wasn't used until later in the war, as well as the fact that Heinrich probably wouldn't have survived his injuries.

Chapter six shows the inside of the HMS Snow. The only real problem is that it's a bit far-fetched that the captain would be passed out, and that there are already plans for the landship.

In chapter seven, we see Hans being tortured, and the crew formulating an escape. They probably would have killed Hans instead of torturing him. The communications post at the top of the ship probably wouldn't have been that simple.

In chapter eight, the crew's plans are finally put into action, leading to the escape of the crew as well as the A7V. This chapter is largely accurate.

Chapter nine sees the crew returning to the Marne. This chapter also lacks notable inaccuracies.

Chapter ten is where one of my most controversial decisions takes place. Why would I add this into my book? Well, I have a few reasons. First of all, it's humanity. It's only human to do what Hans did. I didn't write it to be dirty and inappropriate. The second reason was realism. It was not uncommon for soldiers to engage in this activity, especially after facing the horrors of the trenches. So it was historically accurate to write about it. The third reason was for the reader. The scene provides the reader with excitement, wondering how Hans will react to the situation he is thrust into and the hope for love in Hans's future. This scene also appeals to some of my older readers, who have been educated about this.

In chapter eleven, the crew is reunited with the A7V, and they hold off the Entente at the Aisne. Now, the inaccuracy here is the tanks that the crew fights weren't made until 1915.

Chapter twelve brings the crew to the Middle East, where they escape an armored train. There is no rail system going from Ypres to the Middle East, and there really is no reason why the French didn't kill the crew.

Chapter thirteen sees the crew making contact with the Ottomans. This chapter lacks inaccuracies.

In chapter fourteen, the Ottomans struggle to hold back the British, and the crew faces dehydration. It's only a bit far-fetched that the British men weren't killed earlier by other soldiers when they sneak into the Ottoman trenches.

In chapter fifteen, the horses probably wouldn't have had explosive dummies on them. The strange thing is, despite being a long chapter, no inaccuracies immediately come to mind.

Chapter sixteen sees the crew returning to Western Front, but the crew's chances of surviving the cold to get there would be low at best.

Now, for chapter seventeen, I can assure you all that the Christmas Truce of 1914 was, in fact, real.

There we go. I'm afraid this book has come to an end. I just want to mention one last thing.

There will be a sequel.

Acknowledgements

I would like to thank my parents and all of my friends for supporting me throughout my life, especially Liam Van der Hagen, Jack Voller, Carter Eisenschenk, Raymond Vanheel, Brandon Moritz, Tyler Salzer, Nick Merdan, Josie Bierbaum, Allie Hoffmann, Alli Hahn, and Anna Scherping. I would also like to thank all of my teachers, especially Mrs. Peschel, Mr. Evan, and Mr. Kvistad. Your kindness gave me the determination to write this book.